The Middle Man

The Brian Konrad Series, Book One

A Novel by DJ Hamlin

Northern Star Publishing, Minneapolis, Minnesota

Northern Star Publishing, LLC 2019
KDP Publishing, 2019
Copyright 2019 by DJ Hamlin

Series: Author D.J. Hamlin, The Middle Man, Book 1 of the Brian Konrad Series. Historical Fiction, 1st Edition.

Paperback ISBN 13: 978-1-7332796-0-4

eBook ISBN 13: 978-1-7332796-1-1

THE MIDDLE MAN

Chapter One

"How in the hell did I get into this mess?" - Brian Konrad

He stood on the marble steps of the museum, the late autumn chill biting at his neck. Pulling his flimsy cotton topcoat collar up and close, he fought off a shiver that ran down his back. The young man lit a Pall Mall, took his first drag of warm tobacco smoke, and felt relief flood through his system. The gray park across the street seemed as lonely as he was...October in Minneapolis was a bitch.

Traffic on the boulevard was uncharacteristically slow, anyone with an ounce of common sense would choose to stay home on this evening, the warmth of a cozy hearth would be welcome and would dull one's senses. He couldn't afford to have his senses compromised. Things were getting riskier every day and the curator had no idea of what might happen next.

One could never be too careful... how in the hell did I get into this mess? he wondered with fear as he finished the cigarette and crushed it out on the ornate marble to his left. *Get a hold of yourself Konrad, you're being paranoid again.*

The alarm that had been triggered suddenly fell silent. He had set if off on purpose again for the third time this week. It was an inconvenience for the night watchman; it was supposed to be. He waited for a few more seconds and pulled his coat tighter around his body, longing for the heat from the lobby behind him. After taking a quick gaze at the park, the young curator consciously shivered and then turned, pushing the large glass door open and feeling the rush of warm air on his face as he moved back inside the building to finish up.

"Hello Mr. Konrad, how are you this fine evening?" The low, manly voice echoed off the interior of the dim lobby.

"Doing well Loren, how are you?" Brian replied with a bit of surprise and relief at the familiar voice.

"Oh, you know, just another night on duty…quiet as can be. Except for that damn alarm up on three…it keeps going off. You wouldn't know anything about that, would you boss?"

The veteran security man gave his reply with a tone of boredom and loneliness, yet also hinted that he knew the answer to his own question. Konrad just smiled, a simple response from a complicated man.

"Say Loren, I've got a question that maybe you can help me with. What do you think of me moving my office down here to the entryway? The security system is constantly being tripped by me after hours...I'm kind of sick of resetting it and I'm sure you don't like answering the alarm either. What do you think?"

The guard looked down at his shoes and slowly kicked his right one forward slightly on the marble floor.

"I suppose it's possible sir. There isn't much in the way of room down here though...you could barely swing a cat through here." Loren smiled at this own comment, meant to bring a little humor to his boss. Brian paused for a moment to let the idea sink in with the guard.

"Well, there is the small alcove over there. With a little construction work I think I could make it work."

The museum curator stalled again for a moment; this decision was already made in his mind.

"You know, most of my work is done out on the floor or upstairs in the administrative conference room. I don't need much space to complete all of my paperwork or article writing. I think it would work very well." Loren nodded dutifully at his boss; he could tell that the decision was as good as made.

"As you say, sir." With his affirmation, the guard continued on his duty rounds in the quiet building.

Although Brian hated the chilling weather that was rousting the last of the fallen leaves across the cement walk, he did enjoy working late at the museum. A night owl for most of his life, he always seemed to come alive after the front doors of the building were locked and his employees were gone. Moving with a quick step to the corner, he looked back at the hulking white edifice lit up for the prominent citizens of the neighborhood.

The young man took exceptional pride in his position and his work. Being one of the youngest museum curators in the country at 30 years of age, his privilege was the product of hard work, a strong education at Columbia University, and the luck to have interned with one of the greatest curators in America.

Brian quickly crossed the intersection at the light and proceeded up Third Avenue a block to his brick Tudor abode. A lit fireplace would feel incredible on this evening. He had actually knocked off early tonight, if one could consider eight o' clock early. Most evenings he would be working until eleven or midnight, would shuffle home to six hours of sleep, and after a quick breakfast of toast, jam, and coffee would be back in his office by seven thirty am.

He was a workaholic and he would be the first to admit this fault, but in his mind, it was a strength. *If you want to be successful and enjoy the finer things in life, you have to put in the work for it.* The young man would repeat this mantra over and over. Everything he had was acquired through hard work and a bit of luck. His story line to his colleagues usually included his undergraduate exploits at Yale and doctoral success at Columbia, but most of his colleagues knew very little other than this. Brian was a quiet person who would prefer to keep to himself.

Chapter Two

"She could be trouble...." - Brian Konrad

The morning arrived a little too early. *I shouldn't have had that second scotch.* Brian pondered this as the noisy, bubbling percolator brewed his morning coffee. The scent hit his nostrils as he spread strawberry jam on his toast, the coffee would give him just the kick he needed. The morning weatherman on WCCO was overly cheerful with his weather report. The Twin Cities operated on the news from this prominent, long time radio station. Konrad figured out within the first week of living in Minnesota that if you were to know what was going on, you had to tune into 'CCO.

Last night's drizzle and cold would give way to a sunny day with a high temperature of 73 degrees, a veritable heat wave compared to the 50's of the last week. November was approaching. *I don't want to have to buy candy for Halloween this year...maybe I should go out.* The young man wasn't one for ghoulish tradition, or any tradition for that matter. The perking noises stopped with a hiss and Brian moved with eager grace to the counter and poured a hot cup. *No need for cream and sugar today, this is going down strong...all the better to fight the scotch.*

The radio now spewed out the trivial news of the day for the city. There was really nothing of interest for the young professional, just the local gossip of which he would not succumb to. Glancing at the clock on his kitchen wall, a realization that he was running fifteen minutes late actually shook him to attention. *Better get there by seven thirty or the staff will have no direction, they will lazy it up.*

Grabbing his gray herringbone blazer, he downed a quick gulp of coffee and cursed himself for not realizing it would be too hot to drink. Dribbling some down his chin, he leaned forward and let the remainder hit the linoleum floor. With an athletic sidestep he left the mess on the floor with a mental note to clean it up later…maybe the cat would lick it up.

"Damn it, cat food…" Brian grabbed the bag from under the sink and dumped a pile next to the spilled coffee. *"Two for one"* he laughed as he thought out loud. "Here Tuffy…come and get it." The cat entered the room with a quizzical stare and slowly moved toward his treat. Brian was out the door with his blazer and briefcase, moving at a slow jog.

"Seven fifty-two, some curator I am, can't even get to work on time."

Truth be told, no one cared except him. Despite his air of self-importance, his underlings needed no direction. As a matter of fact, many of the museum employees under his watch really had little to do with him. The museum functioned very well before him and would probably continue to function very well after he was gone. Everyone who had been working there for any extended period of time would know exactly what they had to do…the MMA functioned like a well-wound timepiece. Always dependable, always dignified.

"Annie, could you get Bill Weber on the line. As soon as possible please?" the curator directed to his secretary. Annie was Mary Anne Rogers, an attractive twenty- seven-year-old woman who had recently divorced her husband of five years. After an abusive situation where she was babysitting a raging alcoholic, a quiet divorce was arranged.

With no children involved it should have been easy, but the stigma of a divorce was hard to fight in this conservative Midwestern enclave. She felt fortunate to keep her job when the news leaked out; the stodgy Republican and Democrat donors could not let anything tarnish the reputation of their beautiful marble masterpiece. The movers and shakers of the jet set made sure that everything that glittered was gold in their institutions, the Minnesota Museum of Art was no exception.

"Yes, sir Mr. Konrad. I will get him on the line immediately." she purred with a soft voice that was pure seduction.

Annie had met Brian at a reception in his honor in late August of 1950 at a plush estate on Lake Minnetonka; she was smitten with his looks and sophistication immediately. Her mission was simple, she was to be the future Mrs. Konrad and go on to have three or four little Konrads and live in fine luxury as someone of great importance in the city.

Brian caught the tone of her voice and it sent a wave of excitement through him, but he had to resist her charm. *There is no time for womanizing and she could be trouble, after all, hasn't she just gotten divorced from her first husband?"* He put that thought on hold as the phone on his desk rang. Not one to waste time, he picked up half way through the second ring.

"Konrad." An air of importance hung with his name.

"Hey boss." the gravelly voice responded.

"Hello Bill, can you come up to my office as soon as possible? I have a new project for you."

Bill was a burly man who had spent the better part of the last twenty- five years working in construction. By default, he had worked his way into leadership with the museum crew. Lacking any kind of real motivation, he rolled his eyes as he listened to his boss.

"Yeah boss, what can I do for you?" he offered with a very small degree of enthusiasm.

Konrad knew the foreman was lazy and crude, but he could build a display or exhibit better than most of the men on the New York crew that he had supervised. No motivation, in fact lazy with a capital L, but he was good with a hammer or paint brush.

"We're going to create a new office in the alcove off the main entryway downstairs. This will be my office; it will not be an easy task. Can you meet me down there in about ten minutes?" There was a degree of urgency and leadership in the young man's voice, Bill knew he meant business.

"Sure thing, boss. See you downstairs in ten." the workman replied with a degree of courtesy. He needed this job to support his wife and five kids, four of which were in college or on the verge of high school graduation. This gig paid well and he was no idiot. If the boss tells you to move, you move.

The area for the new office sat just to the right of the main entry to the museum. When Bill was told of the plan on the spot, a quizzical look fell over his face. Brian noticed this strange look of doubt and assured the workman that the office would be very functional. After a half hour of inspecting and designing within the space, both men agreed that the office was very possible. A timeline was established that would have the curator in his new office within two weeks. The first week of November would be perfect for Brian and his plan.

****

"Miss Rogers, could you bring the personnel files from the fourth-floor office to our conference room as soon as possible? They are in the top drawer of the cabinet, a red file with a label that says RESUMES."

Annie turned to her friend Kit, a fellow employee, and put a finger in front of her dark red lips to signal quiet. Her friend's expression suddenly turned to one of puzzlement, but she kept silent.

"Yes sir, Mr. Pemberton. I will bring those to you right away."

The lead secretary placed the phone back on its cradle and remained silent for another moment to be sure the line was clear.

"What in the world was that all about?" her friend asked with trepidation.

"Oh, it's no big deal. Pemberton and the board are looking to hire an assistant for Mr. Konrad."

Kit caught herself smiling at the mention of the curator, but quickly hid her interest knowing that Annie had the hots for the boss.

"Wait a minute...aren't you the assistant to Mr. Konrad?"

The lead secretary smiled and gauged her reply carefully.

"Um...as of right now I am, but who knows what the future brings?"

"I know what you would like it to bring!" the excited friend couldn't hold back the comment and both women laughed.

"Well, we will see about that." was the only cautious reply that Annie could muster. "Let's go get Mr. Pemberton his files."

Both women rose, crossed the marble corridor to the elevators, and made their way to the administrative offices on the top floor of the museum. The only noise that echoed through the expanse of exhibits was the clicking of high heels on marble.

Annie found the key on her crowded ring despite the lack of proper lighting in the narrow corridor and both women ducked inside the personnel office quickly. The lead secretary flipped the light switch next to the door and the fluorescent bulbs began to hum as a bright, yellow light flooded the room. The eerie quiet of the vacant office sent shivers down their spines and both women turned their gazes toward each other.

"It's scary as hell up here, right?" Kit whispered, adding a spookiness to the room.

"You know they say there are ghosts up here, right?" Annie retorted with a low whisper of her own.

"Knock it off!" Kit insisted in a high pitch, her voice echoing back into the corridor to places unknown. She delivered a playful punch to Annie's bicep and both women burst out in nervous laughter.

"Let's see. It should be right over here. Yes, top drawer." Annie slid the heavy, metal drawer open and the files were at the front, an easy find. Kit looked around her friend and quickly snatched a file from the middle of the drawer.

"Well, well...what do we have here? Mr. Brian Konrad's personnel file!" She pivoted away from the drawer quickly, keeping the file away from her friend.

"Kit! Give that back! If I get caught with his file I could be fired!"

The friend was wearing a sly smile; she knew of the danger but wanted to read up on the handsome, available curator.

"They will never know. We take this to your desk on the way to the conference room, deliver the files to Pemberton, and then read up on Mr. Dreamy. We can put Konrad's file back when we return the others. No harm done, right?"

Annie gave her partner in crime a disapproving glare, but the temptation was too much.

"We had better NOT get caught!"

Kit smiled and led the way out of the office with a triumphant gate.

Locking the door behind them, they moved quickly to the elevator and, after leaving the special file in Annie's top drawer, they proceeded to deliver the requested files to the top boss. After quickly excusing themselves from the board room, they could barely conceal their eagerness to delve into Brian Konrad's information.

One of the many downfalls of not having an office of your own is that there is no privacy. Both women found themselves looking around for intruders as they perused the files with glee and curiosity. They began conversing in low voices, sharing the forbidden secrets.

"Says here that he graduated with honors from NYU and Columbia...a New York man!" Kit stated with an air of attraction. "Internship at the Museum of Modern Art in New York City...worked for a Dr. Andrew Brooks, must be a big shot. There's even a letter of recommendation from him." They were both silent for moment, working through more information.

"He is NOT married! Just as I expected."

Annie couldn't hold away the smile that now covered her face and Kit smiled back.

"I know THAT look! That's the Mrs. Brian Konrad look!" The lead secretary's smile turned to a blush and her friend laughed at her correct assessment.

"Seriously, Kit...why would he marry me?"

"You're kidding, right?" Kit displayed an expression of mock astonishment as she kidded her friend.

Annie smiled again to herself, a confident feeling a warmth welling up inside of her.

Annie pulled out a page of the personnel docket and continued her detective work.

"Interviewed last spring. Hired in July of 1950, he started after Labor Day. No surprises here...we already know this, nothing special. Say, did you know he lives right down the street from here?"

Kit was trying to mess with her friend as she responded "I already knew that...been there already." Annie found the humor in her statement and wasn't about to fall for it.

"Katherine, shame on you!" The friends let out a shared giggle as they carefully placed the documents back into the manila folder.

Chapter Three

"no turning back now..." - Brian Konrad

The package arrived in a crate the size of a small toaster. Stamped with the insignia of the New York Museum of Modern Art, it had been eagerly anticipated on the loading dock by Brian. In fact, the boss had been checking the incoming schedule every morning for the past ten days. With Thanksgiving fast approaching, Konrad began to worry that something was wrong. Then, with almost all hope gone, there it was...the small brown package.

After signing the delivery in as an artifact for display, Brian took the elevator to the second floor where his office was. At the MMA, the large stone steps ornately led you to the second- floor main entry of the museum, a grand climb that made one's visit seem much more important.

The curator's new office sat off to the side of the main entry, all the better to inspect and greet visiting dignitaries and donors. Brian Konrad's name was officially displayed in gold lettering on the opaque glass door for all to see. With the door closed no one had to know how tiny and cramped this space was.

After hastily clearing a spot on his worn, dark oak desk he carefully opened the package. As Brian was discretely peeling the wrapping paper off the box there was a gentle knock on the door. He had become accustomed to the sound; Annie was outside. Moving the box to the floor behind his desk he muttered with tired authority "Come on in."

Annie opened the door and caught his eye right away in her dark skirt and white blouse. She was a striking woman and most of the male employees and visitors tried in vain to catch her attention, but she only had eyes for the curator and he knew it. He couldn't contain a smile as she stood in the doorway.

Brushing her auburn hair back with a seductive flip of her dainty hand, she looked at Brian and smiled. "I was wondering... with our post-modern exhibit about over, what do you have planned next?" Brian leaned back, not ready for the question and less enthusiastic about the answer.

The beautiful secretary sensed this right away and not wanting to create an uncomfortable situation quickly added "Edward Allen called wondering if he could get bank sponsorship for the next showing. I figured you should have a heads up before he approaches you next week. He is hosting a gala for a program at the U and you will be invited...he called to extend the invite himself this morning but you were busy."

"Interesting. I wonder why he would invite me to something outside the art world?" Brian thought aloud.

"Come on, Brian. You're the next big thing. You know I think so anyway." she replied coquettishly, judging his response. Taken aback but flattered, his face started to redden as she continued. "Who are you going to go with? Assuming you will go, of course."

The opening to his asking her was suddenly right there; should he take the chance?

"I would need a date, wouldn't I? It wouldn't be proper to attend something so important, so dignified, without a lady, would it?" He smiled and looked her over with the kind of admiration that a man gives a beautiful woman.

"The results could be tragic if one were to show up alone, right?" she retorted with a look of mock consternation.

This look was suddenly mirrored on Brian's face as well. Taking off his wire rim glasses and gently biting the earpiece, he looked Annie over. *Absolutely beautiful...out of my league, but what the hell, why not?*

Assuming a stoic tone, he asked "So what is the date of the gala?"

With a serious tone she replied "Mr. Allen requests your presence on the tenth of next month, the gathering will be at his house over on East River Road." He let the silence linger for a moment, creating a scene of anticipation.

"So, Annie, what might you be doing on the tenth of next month?" he inquired with a playful interest.

"Well sir, at the moment I have no plans." she cooed back with an interest of her own.

"Would you do me the honor of accompanying me to the gala at the Allen estate?"

A tense moment followed but he was quickly reassured of her feelings. "I would be delighted." The response came with an excited but reserved smile.

Annie pivoted, giving Brian a chance to check her out as she exited the room. *This could be good!* It took a moment for the young man to regain his composure and return to the business at hand.

The valued container was again placed on the plain, cluttered desktop and with a minimal effort Brian peeled the end open. Inside the wrapped cardboard container was a wooden slat board box. Grabbing a scissors from his desk drawer, he pried the top slat apart from the rest of the thin, pine boards and the mini-crate opened up. Moving padded packing paper aside he studied the contents carefully.

Inside the package were two small vases, foreign looking and very old. He was hesitant to pick them up for a moment, then realized that few people even knew of their existence. This made him even more nervous. The second vase he removed was the one with the information inside. Taped to the inner surface, out of view, was a note and a small piece of microfiche. Both were in a small cylinder used for holding camera film. He opened the black container and fished out the note.

K,
Hope this finds you well. All is a go here, things good. Display none of contents. Send to DMOA, care of JF. Contact to come, keep film. Return should arrive by holiday 25, send back. Talk soon,
ABE.

"Wow, this is it... everything is underway... no turning back now."

Beads of sweat formed on his brow and he removed his glasses and rubbed his eyes with his free hand. The vases were to proceed to James Fishel at the Denver Museum of Art, the microfiche was to be passed on to someone else at a later date. They would apparently contact him for the drop, he had no idea what was on the film and frankly did not want to know. He was a conduit in this game and wanted nothing else, he was loyal to ABE. Andrew Brooks, Esquire would be contacting him soon, hopefully at home.

Brian needed a break, he felt overcome with stuffiness inside his small office. Grabbing his pack of Pall Malls, he snagged his topcoat off the rack and headed out the front doors of the museum. A busload of kids from an elementary field trip were unloading at the bottom of the steps; the whole exercise seemed to convey nothing short of total chaos. He had no longing for that kind of interaction and steered clear as he descended down the left railing on his way to the park.

The mid-morning sun hit him square across the back as he left the shadow of the building at the bottom of the stairs. He had no need of the coat; it was much warmer compared to when he had arrived a few hours earlier. Flipping the garment across one arm, he settled on a bench in the park across the street and lit a cigarette. The smoke filled his lungs and wafted upward as he exhaled, the experience calming him from the start. *Thank goodness for Pall Malls...can't survive without them.*

The yellow bus on the other side of the street pulled away as a heavy-set elementary teacher led her entourage of unrulies up the steps. *"A damn nightmare. Why in the world do we let the monsters in? Something will surely get trashed...they have neither the manners or the maturity to even be here."*

Konrad found a sudden hatred boiling up inside him. Another drag on the cigarette changed his focus from the troop of elementary kids to Annie Rogers. *"What a dream...I could really see myself with her."*

Being a modern man with a healthy appetite for the opposite sex, he suddenly focused on the possibilities he might have. Brian looked around, feeling a sense of embarrassment and slight shame as he thought of his secretary in a lustful manner. A gentleman was not supposed to reflect on such things but Brian was a man, pure and simple. She was stunning, too good not to think about. His shame was replaced with a sly smile as he realized that he might have a chance with this beautiful woman.

Break time was over. There were too many pressing issues and too many things to accomplish; the young curator could not afford to waste precious time gazing across the busy street. The boss made his way back to work, hastily gliding up the stone steps two at a time.

Being a man of slender build, he had no problem staying in shape. His membership at the Minneapolis Athletic Club was seldom used, he actually felt uncomfortable in this social setting, and yet he somehow managed to stay trim and fit.

Good genes, great lineage. He almost congratulated himself on this luck. In reality, none of his colleagues here knew anything about his upbringing and he made sure they would not find out.

He would brag to anyone curious about his past that he was from New England's finest. The truth was much less grandiose. Brian had actually grown up just north of the Bronx in New York City. His education was nothing to brag about until he was suddenly accepted into Columbia University on the recommendation of some very important people. New York aristocrats had come to his aid after he became involved in a young gentleman's club on the Upper East Side.

A classmate from his high school had gotten involved in a social committee that fed into a club of activists calling for a more liberal agenda with the government. The rhetoric, the belonging, the mission for change was all that he had needed; he suddenly became aware and had a purpose. Now he was an agent for change, part of the real world. Nobody could know the real history of Brian Konrad; it could be deadly.

Entering the marbled front portico of the museum, Brian made sure to wander around the corner and check out Annie one more time before he had to return to the package on his desk. Her post was empty, she must have been out on the floor guiding the youngsters through exhibits. He returned to his cubby hole of an office and repackaged the vases in the small crate. Within two minutes the parcel was ready to forward to Denver.

Quickly typing up a shipping slip, he fastened it over the Minneapolis destination marker and walked the goods back down to the shipping room. A mostly full mail truck was pulling out of the dock as he opened the swinging doors. The bright, fresh air and vibrant sounds of the street hit him as he sauntered up to two of the idle shipping clerks on the rail.

"Hello Emery. Could you do me a favor and get this out today if possible? It's headed for Denver and they are in a rush out there...I guess they have been expecting it for a while. I already typed up the shipping tag."

The young, smallish clerk smiled at his boss, eager to please him. "No problem Mr. Konrad. I will get it out this afternoon."

"Thank you, Emery. I can always count on you."

The shipping clerk beamed with the realization that he was in favor with the highest man on the totem pole. Brian felt a wave of relief wash over him. Nobody would check the contents of the package. He was home free in regard to this task and it felt good to be working for the cause. Turning lightly on his heels, he decided to pass Annie's desk on the way to his office.

She was there. Her eyes met his and there was a certain gleam that told him she was interested in him.

"Say Annie, got a minute?"

"Sure boss, what do you need?" Brian was not suave with the female gender, but he suddenly felt empowered in her presence.

"I was wondering, what are you doing tomorrow night?"

Annie moved slightly upright, startled by this question. "Um, I don't really have any plans. Why?"

Her lips suddenly formed a knowing smile of what might come next. "Have you ever been over to the Monte Carlo Club before? I was thinking that maybe we could have dinner…"

She interrupted him mid-sentence with a nod. "I could be ready at seven?" A warm grin now overcame his face.

"I will pick you up at seven then." the young man declared with confidence. *Could the day get any better?*

Chapter Four

"Never mix business with pleasure...isn't that a golden rule?" - Brian Konrad

The morning sun drifted in through the curtains, cascading down upon his face. The warmth felt really good; he felt like he was slowly rising from a very deep dream. Brian casually rolled over and opened his eyes. A moment of surprise hit him as he gazed upon the sleeping face of Annie. Surprise was replaced in his mind by sublime happiness.

He admired the curve of her face, her lovely long red hair laying across her soft, white shoulders. Asking for the date was an accomplishment in itself, Annie spending the night was beyond anything he could have expected. A splendid dinner at the classic restaurant led to after dinner drinks at their stylish bar and then there was the cab ride home that led to a few more nightcaps followed by a passionate interlude.

Annie moaned slightly in her sleep and moved closer to him. Her hand reached out and caressed his chest as she slowly opened her eyes.

Hi." she whispered shyly, not knowing how he would react. Brian smiled and kissed her on the forehead as she snuggled over to him.

"How are you?" he whispered back, hoping her reply would be favorable.

"Wonderful." she cooed with a smile, judging his reaction.

At that moment both of them realized that they were now a couple. How he would deal with this situation left him without a clue. The curator and his secretary were now an item and he really didn't care about anything else. With a smile from ear to ear, he held her like he would never let her go.

Saturday meant a day off for the lovebirds. Brian made sure that he never had to work on the weekends and if he didn't have to work, Annie didn't have to work either. They spent the weekend together at his house and when Sunday night arrived, she returned home. Five minutes after Annie left his front door, Brian suddenly felt cold and lonely. The reality of the situation sank into his mind. Earlier feelings of contentment now turned to panic.

Pouring himself a scotch and lighting a cigarette, he dropped into a comfortable chair in his living room. The cat settled at his feet, unaware of the trouble in its owner's mind.

Never mix business with pleasure, isn't that a golden rule? Don't get caught up in her, it can only turn out bad. Don't hurt her, she's too special for that. How can I let her down? Why can't I have her and everything else too? She will understand when I explain it all to her.

The smoke and alcohol slowly took hold of his mind and he mellowed out. There was no way he could let her go, he would have to tell her sooner or later about himself and what was going on. Later would be better, much later. The gala would be next week, after the Thanksgiving holiday. Another date could solidify things, although realistically he felt they were now going out.

People would recognize him with Annie on his arm and he would be elevated to a whole new level of status. Men would admire him for the beautiful woman he had acquired, women would look to him with a new level of admiration while wishing they could be his. This situation was a win-win all around; he gets the girl and he gets the glory. No one would ever suspect him now as he had the perfect cover story.

****

A light dust of snow ushered in the national holiday and Americans across the country sat down with their families to celebrate. Neither Brian or

Annie had any real family to enjoy Thanksgiving with and so they spent the day at his home. The new couple now had a chance to enjoy the break from work with each other and so they spent their time reading, playing games, and listening to the radio. Annie enjoyed the chance to finally take care of her man without the pressures and violence of an abusive relationship.

Things finally seemed right for both of them and they reveled in the company of one another. Brian couldn't remember the last time he had been this happy. Being a man of quiet solitude had its benefits but as he slowly moved toward middle age this felt much better. The new couple came to the realization that they could accept each other for who they were, no facades, and both were falling in love. It was good to have someone to take care of you.

Friday morning signaled the end of an interrupted work week due to the holiday, but Konrad knew that things would be different. The visitors would be more reserved as families and mostly adults would be their clientele. No school buses full of raging little savages would descend upon the museum, a day like this would epitomize what the MMA really existed for. Eager and happy, Brian arrived early and made his first inspection rounds of the floors, starting at level one and working his way up.

"These exhibits look really sharp. Say what you want about Bill's attitude, but his crew really does one hell of a job. About as perfect as you can get." the young curator

muttered to himself. *"I will have to make a note to send him regards for a job well done."*

The latest exhibit was upstairs on the third floor and featured artists from the early to mid-twentieth century who specialized in Dadaism, a unique art form.

Many people found this type of art bizarre, to some it looked like pictures cut apart and put back together wrong. Some pieces looked too strange to interpret, almost scary. Brian found this art form especially pleasing, it made each person interpret and think; this was the type of art he had learned to like in New York.

Eastern Europe and the Soviet Union were turning out some of the greatest pieces of art in this genre and he knew he could acquire some of the finest items. The loading dock downstairs was filled every day with the latest shipments from Eastern Europe by way of Paris or London. Andrew Brooks would ship the pieces west from New York with the latest information tucked inside for inspection by the curator. Brian would keep some of the choice pieces and send the rest on to Denver or Santa Fe. A note would accompany the piece of art and all would be good.

It was the latest piece that really caught his attention and piqued his curiosity. ABE had sent a framed piece that looked almost demonic in nature. Brian wondered if he could even display it in the museum. Most of the Midwest art admirers would think it too scary to appreciate.

A small note was taped to the back, facing into the portrait. The curator knew enough to expect some sort of message and this time was no exception. The note contained a phone number for the Twin Cities area with a message to call on the first day of the new month; December first. Summit 1869 was a St. Paul number from a well to do neighborhood.

"Who in the world would this be?" Konrad wondered quietly to himself. The painting was shipped on to Denver. *"Let them worry about this weird thing...I have what I need."*

Chapter Five

*"Well, well, if it isn't The Boy Wonder..." - Miss
Evelyn*

The evening of the gala had finally arrived. This was
the social event of the season leading into the
Christmas holiday. Every newspaper in town
featured a spread on this sumptuous happening.

The Allen family was well known for their
business savvy and philanthropy, they were among
the cream of the crop in the social circles of the state.
Need something done, a cause funded, the ear of the
governor, all you had to do is buddy up to and ask an
Allen. The exhibit at MMA that featured Dadaism
was sponsored by the Allen family foundation. Big
money was put up to rent the pieces that were now
on display and a certain percentage was making its
way back to the Upper East Side of New York City.

Brian Konrad arrived on this prestigious evening
with Annie Rogers on his arm. They made a striking
couple; the studious but handsome introvert and his
stunning, outgoing date.

Brian was not big on these types of social functions; in fact, he would be the guest that one would find hanging out in a garden or library alone while everyone else socialized and danced. It was an aspect of his job that he truly did not enjoy but knew he had to capitulate to …he had to take one for the team so to speak. The money, the connections, the show were what would make both him and the museum successful.

Somewhere in the middle of the evening Brian got separated from Annie in the midst of all the social chaos. Retiring to a side room in the luxurious mansion, he allowed himself a moment to let his mind catch up with the events and people of the evening. If he had to try and remember one more name of a rich socialite he was probably going snap and kill the guest.

With fatigue clouding his mind, he failed to notice the sexy brunette enter the room until she was six feet away. Evelyn Pomeroy startled him and he almost spilled his drink on the overly expensive rug.

A rumored relative to the famous Minneapolis milling fortune, this five-foot one-inch bundle of dynamite attracted all the attention wherever she went. Evelyn didn't walk into a room, she floated into it and commanded the notice of everyone in her presence. Brian realized in the first ten seconds that even if he couldn't identify her by name, he wasn't about to carry through on his threat to kill. She was just too beautiful to ignore and he felt he should know her from somewhere.

"Well, well, if it isn't the boy wonder from the Minneapolis art scene." Her voice was soft and seductive; Brian was enamored with her immediately.

"I wouldn't go as far as to say that." he replied with a quiet laugh. He suddenly noticed that they were the only two in the dark paneled, dimly lit room.

"I have heard it said that you are the youngest curator in the country. My uncle says that you're displays are brilliant. I saw the new one last week and I have to say that I was NOT impressed."

Evelyn was teasing him, trying for a reaction. Brian gave her one.

"I'm sorry the exhibit did not live up to your standards. Apparently, your uncle has better taste in art than you do." This retort drew a cute laugh from the petite beauty.

"My name is Evelyn, my friends call me Evie. I know who you are, everybody who is somebody knows Brian Konrad."

Her flattery was working; Brian could feel the blood rush to his face.

"Oh, my! The boy wonder blushes!" Evie exclaimed with a louder laugh.

Brian suddenly realized she was messing with him and he didn't quite know how to react. She was so bold for such a small woman, yet with short dark hair and mysterious eyes she was gently beautiful. As hard as he could try, he could not stop staring into her eyes. His mind suddenly shifted into gear and he realized that Evelyn was a potential heir to the Pomeroy fortune, one of the largest piles of wealth in the country.

"I'm sorry." she apologized with a more mellow voice. "Sometimes the alcohol gets the best of me."

Searching for impairment, Brian couldn't tell that she had even had one drink. The alcohol had been flowing freely all evening and he had helped himself to a martini or three, but he suspected she had consumed much less. The stare of her mesmerizing eyes never wavered as they both moved slightly closer to each other.

"Don't you just hate these things? Stuffy people with way too much money and so much self-importance. I really can't stand the boring conversation...nobody has anything of value to say. Everybody acts like they are best friends and then tomorrow they will be talking behind each other's backs. Total back stabbers. They will compare bank book balances and sizes of their estates across town, always trying to outdo each other. I won't even get into how they will steal each other's spouses…cheaters, all of them."

Brian realized that Evie really couldn't shut up, she was dominating the conversation but he really didn't care. His fascination with her continued throughout her tirade against her peers.

"So, tell me pretty Evelyn, aren't you just like all of the people you just described?" This rubbed her the wrong way, her smile turned to a fiery gaze of anger.

"Look here! You don't know the first thing about me!" She backed up a step and thrust her chin out at Brian.

He interrupted her quickly. "Hey, take it easy. I'm just kidding around with you!" Her posture lightened up and she regained her composure. After looking away for a moment, then down at her feet, she continued.

"Say, how would you like to come out to the lake for a holiday get together? It will be grand! I must wager that you have never had a time like this! I could send an invitation and you could be my special guest!" Her smile was back and excitement filled her voice.

"And what? Be the target of more of your wrath?" he chuckled with a smile to match hers.

"Look, I'm sorry about the way I came off. Friends?" she offered with an outstretched hand.

Brian offered his hand to her and she pulled her body in close to his. Standing on her tiptoes she embraced him and gently touched her face to his neck. He could smell her perfume and it aroused his senses. Evie's lips gently touched the side of his face with a kiss and he held the embrace, caught up in her passion.

She fell away, rocking back on her feet and looked him in the eyes with a flirtatious smile. "I will be in touch with you, boy wonder." she whispered.

Brian watched her float out of the room and back into the chaos of the gathering. He caught himself breathing heavier than before, his pulse was racing, a very rare reaction for Brian to experience. He couldn't wipe the confident grin off his face.

"What are you smiling about?" The familiar female voice stirred him back into reality.

"Umm, nothing I guess." he replied, suddenly embarrassed.

"Who was that?" she inquired with a dose of suspicion.

"Just an old friend from the past." he lied, hoping the subject would change.

"She's very pretty." Anne offered, hoping to realize more about what had just occurred.

"She's all right I guess...extremely difficult to talk to though. Too many opinions."

An awkward moment shared between lovers; he wanted the conversation to change course quickly. "So, are you having a good time?" he asked with faked concern.

"Yes, a great time! I am amazed at how many of the movers and shakers from the community are here. Everyone who is someone must be here tonight. I honestly did not expect so many important people, I think the governor is even here!"

Annie was enjoying the celebrity status that she had acquired through Brian. He looked at the beauty in front of him and realized that every man in the room would probably die to get the chance to take her home. He was a lucky man. After a little dancing and a little more to drink, they made their way back to Brian's place.

As he slid out of the cab in front of his house, he looked his ravishing date over one more time. A great night was still ahead. While he slid the key into the front door and opened it for Annie a sudden vision of Evie burst into his mind and he paused for a moment as guilt overcame him.

"What's wrong dear?" the lovely Annie inquired, studying her man on the front steps of his house. Brian looked away for a quick second, composed his mind, and locked eyes with the ravishing redhead.

"Nothing dear, absolutely nothing."

His voice was soothing to her, she felt safe and lucky with him. They shared smiles and she moved in to kiss him on the lips, a long kiss filled with passion. The image of the other woman in his head was suddenly gone.

Chapter Six

"Mr. Konrad, I know everything about you…" -
Summit 1869

Monday morning arrived too quickly. The weekend seemed to disappear in a flash and now Brian found his way to the bathroom in a daze. Sleep had been hard to acquire, his mind worked late into the night. Drifting off after surveying the alarm clock for two hours, he didn't actually fall into a deep sleep until well after one in the morning. Five hours of sleep would not cut it; he was going to have a rough day.

After completing his toiletry tasks, he stepped out of the shower and dressed quickly for work. A dark suit with subtle pinstripes, accented by a white dress shirt and light blue tie, he admired his appearance in the mirror on his closet door.

Not bad…not bad at all. They both think I am the real deal…lucky me! His smile returned to him in the mirror as he realized that he was doing very well for himself in most of life's regards.

The usual breakfast of toast, jam, and coffee went down without much thought. The customary radio report droned on like background noise that never really gained his attention. He was slowly waking up and feeling a little better. In the back of his mind there was the realization again that he could have a rough day as sleep deprivation was a known production killer.

The young curator was never one to struggle with sleep. It was the norm for him to drift off to slumber the minute his head hit the pillow. His mind was composed with the help of caffeine, but there was this strange feeling of apprehension and certain dread. One bad moment could send his day into a downward spiral. Spending the weekend with Annie wore him out physically; thinking of Evie wore him out mentally.

For the first time in his life, Brian was having a hard time trying to figure himself out. The infatuation with the stranger at the party on Friday night kept running through his mind. There didn't seem to be a way to get rid of the vision of her…he would have to call her sooner or later.

She did say that she would send a personal invitation to me for a get together out at the lake. The young curator resigned himself to the idea that the only way he would see her again would be if the invite arrived before the holiday.

Nothing wakes a person up quicker than the blast of an icy winter wind mixed with wet snow on a cold Minnesota morning. With the opening of the front door, Brian suddenly realized that the weather had changed drastically overnight. Although there was only a dusting of snow on the front sidewalk, the wind and temperature now announced the formal arrival of winter. With an alarmed curse word Konrad stepped back and quickly slammed the front door shut.

Retreating into the hallway, he opened the closet door and fished around for his formal winter coat. Finding his black full-length overcoat, he slipped it on with an additional shiver and haste. Grabbing his favorite wool hat and a pair of leather gloves from the top shelf, he donned the winter gear and headed for the street with briefcase in hand.

The three blocks that he walked to work seemed to last forever as he fought against a head wind that was determined to keep him from his destination. Taking care to not slip on the icy cement sidewalk, he moved with a cautious purpose and arrived at the museum at seven-thirty sharp. Less than three minutes after his arrival Annie was at his office door with the newspaper and a cup of hot coffee.

"I knew there was a reason that I loved you" he stated with a smile while he took the cup in both hands and enjoyed a healthy sip. The heat from the cup slowly brought feeling back to his fingers.

"Here I thought it was for my body..." she playfully retorted with a whisper to make sure that no one within earshot would hear.

Exchanging smiles, they both looked quickly around to make sure no one heard them or saw their interaction. The office rumors of the new romance had started around the workplace but no one had the courage to actually confirm them with proper questioning. The longer they could keep their relationship secret the better things would be.

Annie was dying to tell her fellow secretary and friend Katherine. Kit had tried to pry information out of her friend, she had suspected there was a spark between the curator and his secretary, but she didn't have the heart or guts to directly ask. She found Brian to be handsome as well and on more than one occasion had toyed with the idea of making a pass on him. He always seemed so aloof, so mysterious.

She now suspected that her close friend had beaten her to the punch. Brian and Annie always seemed to be smiling about some inside joke or situation. Lately they seemed to be a little too close to one another, a little too touchy and feely. Something was going on and Kit feared that Annie had captured the heart of the man that she secretly desired.

After downing the cup of strong coffee, Brian hunkered down in his office and prepared for a busy day. December first... the day that the shipment from New York would arrive. After a tense half hour, he decided to take a walk down to the loading dock on the west side of the building.

"Hello Emery, anything arrive this morning that I should know about? Anything from New York?"

Emery put on his best smile and walked toward his boss. "Yes sir, that wooden crate over there. It's a heavy beast. I can't imagine what's in there." His smile widened as he hoped for an accolade from his role model and boss.

"Emery, I could tell you but I would have to kill you." the curator joked to his employee. Both men laughed and Brian pulled the shipping tag which declared New York as the point of origin and Minneapolis as the point of destination. He carried this documentation up to his office.

"Mr. Konrad? I have a gentleman by the name of Phillip Summers here to meet you. He says he has some questions about funding a new exhibit. Should I send him in?"

Brian shifted the phone receiver against his ear. "Yes Annie, I can see him now. Please send him over." *"A Mister Phillip Summers...who could that be? The name doesn't ring a bell..."*

Konrad rose from his chair at the knock on the door and opened it to find a tall man with a darker, ruddy complexion standing in the doorway with hand extended.

"Mr. Konrad, my name is Phillip Summers." Brian extended his hand to meet the strangers and they exchanged a hearty handshake.

"Hello Mr. Summers, it's a pleasure to meet you. Please come in, make yourself comfortable."

Brian settled into his chair on the opposite side of the worn desk and studied his guest carefully. The middle-aged man gave off an air of importance and wealth. He seemed to be somebody that the young curator should have known, the type of person that you can't quite seem to place but feel that you recognize from somewhere. Summers sat back in his chair and studied the young curator as well. The silence between them suddenly became uncomfortable.

"Can I get you anything? A cup of coffee? A drink?" Brian extended the hospitality with a genuine smile.

"No thank you, I'm fine." Summers replied with a matching expression.

"So, what can I do for you?" Brian offered with curiosity.

"Mr. Konrad, we have some mutual acquaintances in both New York and Denver. I thought it proper that we meet and get to know each other as well. We both have very much in common. I believe that ABE may have told you of my existence here in the cities, is that correct?"

Brian's mind raced back to the earlier shipment from New York and the note that was attached. "Summit 1869, is that correct?" he asked in a more subdued voice.

"That is correct, K." This was the other side of the information contact that Brian had anticipated. Summit 1869, aka Mr. Summers would be providing information of value to the cause and Brian would send it on to the east and his friend ABE.

"Is it ok to talk here?" Summers wondered aloud.

"Today, yes. In the future... not as much." Brian countered. Summers paused for a moment, then resumed.

"I will be delivering information to you twice a month, I do not know which days. Check for a sign every morning around ten o'clock, only during the weekdays. If you look across the street at the park bench near the corner you will see the sign. I will leave a piece of light-colored tape attached to the top of the trashcan next to the bench. If you see the sign be prepared to meet me at ten o'clock in the evening right here. Will it be a problem to meet up here after hours?"

Brian studied his face for a moment, paranoia was sweeping through his brain. This man had to be trustworthy, he knew too much information to not be authentic and sympathetic to the cause.

"Meeting here will not be a problem. We only have one night watchman on duty and he won't suspect anything as long as you are with me. I will go out for a smoking break at nine-fifty. I can let you in at ten. How do I know you are legitimate? We have to be very careful these days."

"Mr. Konrad, I know everything about you...some things that only a person on the inside would know." The older gentleman let his statement sink in for effect. He looked left and right, then lowered his voice.

"I know you studied with Dr. Andrew Brooks...your internship involved more than just Dadaism art. You have been a member of the club since 1947 and your education was secured and paid for by our friends...ABE being the most important. Your move here from New York City was, shall we say, strategic? Is there a need to go on?"

Brian slowly moved his head side to side to indicate the negative; there really was no need to go on and the young curator suddenly felt a combination of guilt and creepiness. He shivered slightly and the agent picked up on the body clue right away.

"Very well Mr. Konrad, it has been a pleasure to meet you. I am looking forward to our work together." The dark stranger rose to his feet with grace and held out his hand for a firm handshake.

"Mr. Summers, the pleasure has been all mine. Feel free to let yourself out and we will meet again soon."

There was a slight hesitation in Konrad's voice that was detected with a smile. With final greetings exchanged, Summers went on his way and the mission became a little clearer to Brian Konrad.

Chapter Seven

"Poor young lady? Hardly!" - Brian Konrad

Brian returned to the paperwork on his desk. He had to set up a new packing slip to keep the merchandise moving west. There was also the delicate task of removing the valuable contents of the huge crate downstairs without anyone detecting anything out of the ordinary. He would have to wait until the museum shut down and everyone went home. As long as he stayed out of the night watchman's way there would be no problem. The best thing he could do would be to carry on with normal business and pick up with this delicate task after hours.

The MMA closed to the public at ten every evening, the night staff was out the door by ten fifteen, and the loading dock workers had left much earlier at six o'clock. The only remaining obstacle was Loren. An average late-night security round would take about forty- five minutes and so, as soon as he passed through the loading area, the coast would be clear. Brian wandered along behind the guard at a safe distance, managed to stay inconspicuous, and entered the loading dock after the friendly guard passed through. The large wooden crate sat off to the side, an obvious priority for tomorrow's staff.

Looking around for a tool, Brian spotted a long-handled pry bar leaning against the wall. With minimal effort, the top was removed quickly and contents were now visible. A tall statue which looked European in origin filled most of the container. A vase about the size of Brian's fist contained a pop-top container of microfiche.

An envelope was attached to the outside of the vase. The curator tucked the container and envelope inside his sport coat and, after placing the top back on the carton and the crowbar back against the wall, moved quickly and quietly back to his office.

Closing the door softly behind him, the curator removed the envelope from his coat and tore off the end carefully as he settled into his chair. Sweat began to form on his forehead and his hands were shaking slightly. Tipping the contents out, he removed an airline ticket to New York and a room key for the Waldorf, Room 505. He paused as a moment of surprise overcame him. The note came out last.

K, expecting you on the sixth of the month, must come quick. News to follow, I will send for you on the eve of the sixth. Travel well and bring container... ABE.

"Container? What container? This one in front of me? The sixth? That's five days away, awfully quick notice..."

Brian was disturbed by the note and contents of the envelope. He fussed over having to leave the museum to travel east on such short notice. Things were too important at MMA; he couldn't just pick up and leave suddenly. The unwritten rule was if ABE told you to do something, you did it without question. There was no room left for freelancing or getting creative on the spot. There was only one leader and that was ABE.

He looked down at the black cylinder of microfiche and inspected the pop top. It was clearly labeled for delivery to DMOA, this wasn't the container described in the note. *"What container...damn it, what container?"*

Puzzled, he began preparations for a trip to New York, checking his desk calendar for notes on the upcoming week. *Not a bad week to be gone...a few field trips, but nothing pressing.* Brian waited for the guard to make his lap and then returned to the loading area.

With the help of a hammer hanging on the wall, he made sure that the top of the container was secure and that the contents looked unopened. It was difficult to properly nail the top into place without making a lot of noise. Throwing caution to the wind, he gave the nails a good beating and then quickly replaced the tools and left the area. The workers would re-open it tomorrow and be none the wiser.

The small vase returned with the curator to the upstairs office where he commandeered a small box and packing material. The film and vase would be tagged with Denver as the destination and would be on their way in the morning.

As for the large statue downstairs, the curator would have to await further directions. He knew better than to display something from New York without proper guidance. This piece was on its way to a private buyer and the container would most probably return full of money instead of the art piece. That wasn't his business, he was just a middle man put in place to keep everything moving safely.

Artwork and directions traveled from New York and, after a brief stop in Minneapolis, would make their way to the west. Atomic secrets and money would work their way back through Brian to his boss in the east. All he had to do was keep everything moving with no detection from government officials. The young curator was beginning to realize the amount of danger he was in.

Fatigue now overtook him, it had been a long day and the timepiece on his wrist indicated midnight. He grabbed his coat, briefcase, hat, and gloves and locked the door behind him. Exiting the building, he checked the door after it closed behind him to make sure it was locked...with a slight clatter he realized it was secure and he carefully descended the steps to the street. He made it home in a next to frozen state and turned in before the clock struck twelve thirty.

The following morning arrived in a cloudy haze. Brian worked to get his mind straight, he couldn't seem to wrap his brain around the events of the day before. This strangers' visit, the large crate, the airline ticket and room key...all of it slowly came back to him. He had made a conscious effort the night before to set his alarm clock for later than usual. An eight o'clock wake up was required if he were to function at all. People would wonder why he was tardy for work, especially Annie, but he could come up with an adequate excuse to cover his extra sleep.

Brian Konrad wasn't the kind of person who could pull off showing up late every day, in fact during his whole professional career he had only done this a couple of times. Today's tardiness was a necessity. As long as he sent the package to Denver before noon, everything would be fine.

As he stepped out into the foggy cold, he could not help but notice the slight feeling of guilt running through him. The last time he felt this remorse he was wondering into a seventh-grade math class with a guilty grin...this ancient memory made him smile as he climbed the steps to his workplace.

After completing his morning museum ritual a little later than normal, Konrad's fellow employees couldn't help but notice the extra spring in his step. Exchanging smiles all around with his staff, everyone's day was brightened and a few staff members traded glances...*things must be going well with the boss and Annie, would wedding bells be in the near future?*

Annie was already hard at work leading groups and answering phones, she seemed busier than normal but took the time to notice that Brian was late for work. Other than at this moment he wouldn't see her for the entire day, a rarity in both of their worlds. As Brian stepped from the elevator onto the first floor, he heard the click-clack of heels on the marble floor. He turned to find the source and was greeted by a pretty smile.

"Hey boy wonder, what's a girl have to do to get a personal tour around here?" she offered with a coquettish tone. Her voice stirred something deep inside of him, a feeling of warmth and confidence overcame his persona. He flashed his handsome instantly and she took note and returned a comely look.

"For you, the world my dear." he delivered in a smooth orators' tone, like somebody taking over the stage in a great drama.

"You look absolutely delicious, my dear." Evelyn was playing on his ego and he was enjoying the flattery.

"And you are beyond stunning!" he returned with a soft tone meant to woo her.

"My uncle is requesting your presence at a party on the fifteenth to celebrate the holiday season. I told him I would personally deliver you myself...you aren't the kind of man to let a poor young lady down, are you?"

The coquettish brunette batted her eyes and stuck out her lower lip in an attempt to be dramatic and cute at the same time.

"Poor young lady? Hardly!" Brian challenged with a smile and a chuckle. "I would be delighted to accept your invitation."

Evie handed him an envelope with a formal invite inside.

"I'm glad you will be attending; I would be lying if I told you that you haven't been on my mind a bit over the last couple of days." This offer of information intrigued Brian even more and he measured a cool response.

"I can relate to your feelings; they are mine also."

She smiled now and not wanting to spoil a good moment chose to make her exit.

"I have to run dear, call me sometime?"

With this invite she slipped a card with her name into his hand and pulled herself close to him. With a soft, long peck on the cheek, her perfume excited his senses. He didn't know what it was but it reeked of wealth…she was quite the woman.

Evie drifted back and pivoted sharply on her heels, looking back over her shoulder to make sure he was checking her out. The curator took notice; her long, black fur coat could conceal some of her curvaceous figure but his imagination filled in the rest of the picture as she held his attention during her whole strut to the door.

She turned, smiled with the devil in her eyes, and waggled her fingers at him in a wave as she pushed out the door into the cold. Brian Konrad was warm all over.

Chapter Eight

"A noble endeavor to save humanity and make the world a better place." – ABE

The eight o'clock flight from Minneapolis to New York took off fifteen minutes late and this really bothered Brian. The late departure of the flight wasn't the problem, the possibility of crashing to earth was the real issue. He fidgeted in his seat and tried to adjust to the noisy interior of the aircraft, but he really couldn't get comfortable.

Cruising along at over three hundred miles per hour, engines stop, plummet to earth and become an instant fireball, people torched to death in an instant as the fireball flies through the cabin, no remains to be identified...

His mind raced through this unlikely possibility over and over and he couldn't get comfortable. *"Why did he have to fly to the east coast, a nice road trip would have been better. Fire up the '48 Buick and see the sights, meet the people..."*

He knew this was never a real possibility, ABE would expect him there on the sixth, no excuses. Everything was set up in fine detail, his boss had it all planned well in advance. Brian had no idea why he was called to the coast, but he had a suspicion. The guest visitor in the wooden carton from earlier in the week had shed new light on this endeavor and now things were getting much more serious.

The guest visitor, in reality a puzzling statue, made its way to from New York to Minneapolis but was not meant for display. This was stolen treasure from somewhere in Europe and it didn't take long to figure out what had happened. Looking back over old newspaper issues, Konrad had figured out the full story.

In the spring of 1942, during the height of the Second World War, the Museum of European History in Austria had suddenly discovered many of its treasures missing. The statue was among the loot that had disappeared, suspected to have been taken by the Third Reich and later confiscated by the Russian Red Army. The valuable stash had never been recovered and suddenly, many years later, the treasure turned up in Brian's museum.

Mr. Summers had shown up the next night, his signal was strategically placed across from the museum and the ten o'clock meeting had taken place. It was simple, actually. Brian would deliver the crate with the statue to the stranger after hours...his men simply pulled up to the loading dock and drove away with the treasure.

When Emery questioned where the crate had gone the next morning, Brian explained that Denver had sent a delivery vehicle and picked up after hours...they were in a rush to get it to a traveling exhibit that was stationed in Des Moines, Iowa and was moving west towards home. Emery never gave the explanation a second thought and the treasure was now on its way to a private owner who had paid big money to own it.

A large crate would be delivered back to the museum the next week and its contents, about one point two million dollars, would make its way back to New York. After New York, it would be on its way to the Eastern Bloc, probably by way of East Germany or Hungary. This part of the plan was way above Brian's pay grade...he kept his mouth shut and did what he was told.

The plane touched down with a thud and Brian felt for a moment like he was going to lose his breakfast. Sweating profusely, he leaned back in his seat as the wicked ride came to a slow crawl and pulled up to a gate. Doors opened, the stairway was moved into position, and Brian did his very best to get out of the plane as quickly as he could. Upon reaching the bottom of the steps he was tempted to kneel down and kiss the tarmac. He wisely resisted this temptation, proceeded inside to gather his suitcase, and directed a cabby towards the Waldorf Astoria hotel off Central Park.

The skyscrapers here were much taller than those in the Midwest and he had to resist looking upwards in wonder. Despite living here for the better part of his life, he never got used to the grandiosity of the big city. It looked different, sounded different, and smelled different than any other place on earth...Brian felt at home.

Settling in to room 505, he unpacked and changed into a dress shirt, suitcoat, and pressed trousers for his meeting uptown. ABE would be expecting him for dinner at the usual location with a formal meeting to follow. His curiosity was piqued, he wondered where the next phase of the plan would take him.

The car arrived at seven and the driver hurried around the auto to open his door for him. After exchanging pleasantries, they moved slowly east toward Fifth Avenue and the organizations' headquarters. Entering from the street into an underground parking area beneath the eight story, block long structure, it took Brian's eyes a moment to adjust.

The car stopped in front of a bank of elevators and Brian passed a formal looking elevator operator with a passing glance. It was understood that the man was really a security agent who had expected his arrival.

"Good evening, Mr. K, it is wonderful to see you again." the husky man exclaimed in a professional manner while doing his best to cover a thick Russian accent.

Brian nodded and smiled but said nothing, it was always safer to say nothing. The elevator doors shut and he was whisked up to the eighth floor. As the doors opened carefully there was another much more menacing looking agent waiting for his arrival. "Please follow me, sir."

The pair walked the better part of a city block, from one end of the building to the other, and said nothing the whole way. Doors lined both sides of the hall and none had any numbers, names, or titles on the placards. Everything was strangely blank. Drab walls, drab carpet, obviously no interior decorator dared to claim this project as their own. The agent carefully swung the double doors open and Dr. Andrew Brooks approached him with a grand smile and a booming voice.

"My son returns! How great it is to see you, young man!" The aged, short but spry man wrapped the young curator in an embrace that threatened to break Brian's ribs.

"Easy now, old man. Don't hurt yourself!" Konrad suggested with a laugh and a smile of his own.

"Tell me, how is life treating you in that great metropolis of Minneapolis?" the leader of one of the greatest museums in the world asked with a mocking air in his voice.

"It's more fascinating than one would think. It's relaxed, yet strangely invigorating." the younger man replied with an air of genuine honesty.

"So, you'll be making it your permanent home then?" Brooks interrupted with a quizzical smile. The old doctor couldn't fathom moving so far away from the bright lights and the action that one of the largest cities in the world would bring.

"I wouldn't go that far, but I do enjoy it for the time being." Konrad countered.

"Let's have a seat...can I get you anything to drink? Vodka, bourbon, scotch? Perhaps a beer?"

"A scotch would be wonderful, on the rocks, please." Brian requested gently, very respectful of his host and mentor.

Brooks turned and nodded to one of his assistants along the side of the room and drinks were delivered in a matter of a minute. The young curator sipped his scotch, its high quality went down with ease. *He would serve nothing but the best...it's all about who you are and what you can have.* Both men took a moment to savor the alcohol and unwind...pleased at their status and company.

"So, now about the business." Brooks wasted little time in getting down to the basis of the meeting. "Things are moving very well; our people back east are very happy. You seem to have settled in with your position and work. Are things as well as they seem?" the old man quizzed, watching Brian's eyes and body demeanor carefully.

"Things are good. We seem to be moving about four parcels a month at this rate...it's still early of course...but no one is the wiser." He took a moment to pause before asking the more important question that had been playing on his mind for the last month.

"How much trouble could I be in if things get discovered, if we get caught? What is it, exactly, that I am doing?" The older man sat back noticeably, taken a little by surprise. Another pause followed as the response was weighed.

"Realistically? The answer depends on what is discovered." A frown came over both men's faces as the air was strangely heavy.

"You have to understand, Brian, that this is serious business. If the government finds out what is being moved, we could all get the chair or rope. Treason, plain and simple. Governments have killed supposed spies for less than this. I presume you heard about Julius?"

The young curator nodded and shifted uncomfortably in his chair, careful not to spill his drink.

"How much trouble could I get in? How am I breaking the law?" Brian looked slowly around the room, studying the rich fixtures, a feeling of nausea and doom coming over him.

I wonder if anyone is listening to us right now? The feds could be in the next room or we could be bugged.

The old man sensed the sudden paranoia in his guest and watched Brian with a curiosity and strange fascination.

"Don't worry, my friend. You are in one of the most secure buildings in the world. There is no way anyone can listen to us, much less even know we are here. We ARE here, right under their noses and they have absolutely no idea! Harry Truman would fall over dead on the spot if he knew about this place!" Brooks let out a hearty laugh that put the young man at ease.

"Haven't you opened any of the crates? The envelopes?" the old man questioned, knowing that Brian had to have at least peaked at what was inside the shipments. Konrad slowly motioned his head back and forth.

"The art going to Denver and beyond is stolen...it goes back to the looting during World War Two.

Nazis grabbed most of it, then we took it from them. The money going back to the east is payment for the contraband. You are, in effect, moving stolen goods and accepting cash under the table." Brian's facial expression grew dark, he didn't like what he was hearing. What he had suspected back home was now confirmed.

"But there's more. Inside most of the art are small documents going west...directives for our people at nuclear testing facilities. When the money or other art pieces come back through your museum they contain microfiche with directions and the latest military secrets concerning nuclear weaponry. These go all the way east...to our homeland." Brian knew he was working for the Soviet regime, but his stomach soured further with this news. The United States government would execute him if he were caught. The young curator broke the silence with a shaky voice.

"I have heard that Julius and his wife are in custody. It appears to me to be a...uh...frame up by the U.S. government. They need a trophy for their efforts to stop the Reds." Konrad took another sip of his drink and rolled the ice cubes in the glass, trying to relax. He had to fight the urge to throw back the remaining alcohol in an effort to numb his troubled mind.

With a quiet but serious tone, the old man worked to reassure his young protégé.

"Julius is in custody, but don't worry, he's hardly a big player. To a certain extent your network is in place to replace his. I would estimate our odds of being discovered with this operation at less than ten percent. Maybe as little as five percent. Not bad odds for what we are doing for our country and the world. A noble endeavor to save humanity and make the world a better place." the old man exclaimed with a confident nod.

"How do you figure?" Brian asked. He knew the answer from his years with the company, but wanted to hear it again from his mentor.

"Think about it. You know the answer. You have trained with us for almost ten years." The old man put down his glass, lifted his left hand, and ticked off the points of his reply with his right index finger.

"First, think of how dangerous it is for the U.S. to be the only one with atomic weaponry. They will run wild with control and exploit the rest of the world. Second, what harm is there in moving products that were confiscated during the war. Someone will profit, it might as well be us. American dollars will strengthen the economy back east. Thirdly, think of all the people still struggling in the east. If you work in the Kremlin you have it made. What about the average people, still devastated by the war? We are rebuilding an economy, a country, and a people. There is great honor in what we are doing."

The argument was incredibly convincing. Dr. Brooks gave credibility to the whole project and Brian could feel his patriotism to the eastern world rising. His head tipped back slightly, his chest out with pride as a smile signaled relief on his face.

Yes, what harm could there be in helping to rebuild lives after the destruction of war. Communism was really a better way for everyone.

Chapter Nine

"Darling, you have arrived!" - Miss Evelyn

A low rumble shook the room as Brian opened his eyes slowly from a very deep slumber. *"Where in the world..."* he wondered mentally as his brain adjusted to his surroundings. A heavy snow was falling in South Minneapolis, having started just before he went to bed. The white precipitation had been falling for hours and was now almost a foot deep.

The rumbling of a snow plow clearing the street had roused him from a dream he couldn't quite remember, and now he sat up slowly and looked out his front window. Everything was grey and white, a pale day made pretty by the huge flakes of snow. Gathering his bearings, Brian realized that tonight would mark the party on Lake Minnetonka that he had been anticipating. He would be Evie's date.

Is it cheating to go to the party with Evelyn? What will Annie do if she finds out? We're really not exclusive, we're not a formal couple, are we?

The questions were starting to flow through his mind as he finished shaving and dressed for the day. They were not living together; in fact, they had seen very little of each other since he returned from New York. Both their lives were just too busy for a social life with each other, and aside from some shared lunches at the museum, they had spent a considerable amount of time without each other.

Annie or Evie? Evie or Annie? Barely know Evie, really like Annie.

His mind messed with him and distracted him from the task at hand, to see how much snow had trapped him inside on this blustery morning.

Tuffy softly patted his way into the kitchen as Brian was finishing the last sip of his first cup of java. "Hey Tuff, wanna go outside?" he questioned with a cruel smile. There was no way the cat would venture into that mess; the snow was taller than he was.

"You're a lucky kitty, you don't have to shovel this crap." The white, fluffy ball of fur turned his head quizzically, wondering what his owner was saying. Brian opened the back door and looked toward the garage.

His '48 Buick was parked inside, but the sidewalk to the garage was at least a foot deep in the heavy white stuff. *"Heart attack snow...shovel it and suffer death."*

The alley looked even worse. The city would run plows down the streets starting with the main routes and then would work their way across the city. They did not bother with alleyways and so it was up to the citizens to shovel and clear a path to drive in. No one had tackled this task yet and Brian was not feeling up to the challenge.

"Where's that damn neighborhood kid when you need him...one dollar and the little punk will shovel the whole alley."

There was no way Brian would shovel today, or any day soon for that matter. It seemed beyond him, there were too many things of greater importance than two hours of physical torture. Thank goodness for the weekends, he would not venture near the museum today. With all this snow, the daily attendance would be light, there would be no school tours on a Saturday and so the staff would sit around bored for most of the day. They did not need him. He did not need to check for the signal from Summit 1869 as they had met the previous day.

No one was the wiser, Summers had walked right in mid-morning and delivered the microfiche as expected. This time Brian made it a point to take a quick look. Pages and pages of documents that had been photographed from somewhere that he couldn't make out. He didn't bother to ask where, he didn't need the pressure of knowing too much.

The package was received and then sent within an art piece to the grand museum in New York. Doctor Brooks would be in possession of the goods by Wednesday at the latest. From there it would take a week or two to arrive in Moscow, no one outside their circle would have a clue.

Konrad stayed in for the day and phoned a couple of acquaintances in town. He didn't really have any close friends; he didn't desire any. Friends just made his life and his many endeavors more complicated. Fellow employees at work would invite him out for drinks and dancing after the workday was complete and he would politely decline. It was easier this way, perhaps that's why he had continued to create more distance between himself and Annie.

He puttered around fixing small things around the house and took a couple hours to peruse the morning Minneapolis Star Newspaper along with a novel he was working his way through. Before he knew it, the time had come to get ready for the party.

Putting on his Sunday best, he donned a sharp, black wool overcoat and headed out the back door to the car in the garage. The snow had stopped and evening had taken over, blessing the new fallen snow with the glitter of moonlight. As he turned from closing the door a shadow caught his eye, if only for a brief second.

Something was there and then it was gone. Too big to be a dog or animal, it seemed human as it drifted behind his garage. He cautiously moved toward the garage, silently cursing the deep snow and called out   "Is anybody there? Can I help you?"

Nobody answered. Being a man of average stature, he wasn't as scared as he was curious. He moved a little quicker and then a thought overcame him.

What if someone is watching me? Do they know? Paranoia overcame him and he stopped in his tracks for what seemed like five minutes. In reality it was probably thirty seconds, but he felt a chill run through him that was not induced by the weather.

Walking around the side of the garage he noted that no one was there. There were no footprints or tracks in the snow, the neighbor kid had shoveled his portion of the alley along with the patch next door. *"A little paranoid?"* he chuckled as he thought out loud to himself.

The garage door opened with its usual clatter, it was supposedly state of the art, one lift and the springs would help push the door up to the ceiling. He found it more disturbing and dangerous than convenient. The Buick started right away and within minutes he was passing the museum as he headed out to Minnetonka.

The modern, fresh suburban area of St. Louis Park was bustling with nighttime activity and he directed the large auto cautiously through traffic. One hour later he was pulling up to the expansive, marble house overlooking the richest lake in the Twin Cities.

As he rounded the circular drive in front of the mansion a valet came to meet him. He left the car running for the uniformed young man and carefully ascended the dozen stone stairs to the front of the house. The door swung open carefully when he reached the top and a butler invited him inside. Brian was prepared to hand him the decorative invitation he had been given weeks earlier but the butler simply admitted him with a smile.

At a party with this level of prominent guests one would not need to present an invite. You were here because you belonged here and those who didn't belong would not be near this event. Turning to his right, he handed his coat and hat to a young girl who was employed simply for this purpose. Konrad entered into a grand entryway full of guests and into another world.

Evie had been looking for him, waiting for his arrival. She had been waiting for this night for weeks now and was glowing with anticipation upon his appearance. Less than ten seconds had elapsed since he had first scanned the room and she was suddenly on his arm.

"Darling, you have arrived!" she squealed with glee as she snuggled up to him. She felt wonderful on his arm and he was enjoying the sudden attention.

He had been waiting to see her also. His demeanor was lifted and things suddenly felt really good. "You look absolutely stunning, Evelyn." he responded with a heartfelt greeting as he gazed down into her dancing eyes.

"We're going to have a wonderful evening. I can't wait for Uncle to meet you!" she replied with a happy eagerness. This would have scared Brian off in any other scenario, the implication that he was her trophy or toy, but tonight it felt absolutely splendid.

They worked their way around the room, spending a better part of an hour drinking champagne and meeting the social elite of the Twin Cities. Anyone who was someone seemed to be in attendance and Konrad would have felt out of place had he not had the beautiful heiress on his arm. She caught the eye of every man in the room with her revealing evening gown and Brian felt a sense of pride as he escorted her from one group to the next.

Evie put on her best charm and had control of every conversation within thirty seconds. It seemed that everyone was taken by her magnetic personality and beauty. Dinner was served at the largest table setting that Brian had ever seen...one of many throughout the dining area and entertainment area. The food was plentiful and beyond the quality that the finest restaurants served; could the night get any better?

Dinner gave way to dancing, entertainment, and more drinking; Konrad was feeling the effects of too much food and drink. Excusing himself to the outer terrace, he found himself alone for the first time all night with Evelyn.

"This is quite the party. It's probably the event of the year." He mused aloud to her, the chill of the air making his breath visible.

"Everybody who is somebody, right?" she answered with a soft smile as their eyes met. The delicate lady gave a soft shiver and Brian removed his suit coat and placed it around her shoulders, much to her delight.

Sensing an intimate moment, he leaned in and gently placed his lips on hers, she gave no resistance and softly moaned. His quest moved to a whole new level as he wondered if he could really be alone with her. Their eyes never left each other; their senses filled with desire.

He placed another passionate kiss on her lips and nodded as if to escape the party guests. Evie sensed this as well and led him back through the main room and, after quickly retrieving their goods from the coat check, out the front door. Hand in hand, they disappeared into the night.

Chapter Ten

"I hate to scare you, Annie, but we are living in strange times." - Brian Konrad

Water, gotta have water. Ouch, where am I? The young man awoke to the sun hitting him directly in the face. His head throbbed uncontrollably and his memory was very unclear. The bed was expansive, decorated in the plushest sense.

"Wake up, wonderful man." Evie whispered as she entered the room from a dressing area.

His memory flooded back to the incredible time he had with Evelyn the night before. No amount of champagne could drown out the wonderful party they had shared.

"I suppose you will get dressed, go home, and never talk to me again, right?" she challenged softly, mostly joking. There was no way he was going to get her out of his head, not after last night.

She slid gently back into bed and into his arms, kissing him with the same passion they had exhibited earlier. He did not resist and continued caressing her, caught up in the next big thing. It was close to noon before they made their way down the staircase and into the main room.

The house was strangely quiet, hired help moving quickly from room to room. This house seemed even larger than the one that well over one hundred guests had celebrated in just hours earlier. The place was absolutely grandiose, it held his gaze as he was mesmerized by the opulent wealth on display.

"Join me for brunch, pleeese?" she giggled, hoping they could spend the day together. Brian was tempted to stay but realized that he had to get back home and get his mind together...this was too much too fast.

"I have to go... I have a busy day. Can I take a rain check on brunch and take you out on the town instead?"

Evie frowned, but then excitement returned to her face. "I would love that!"

One more long, passionate goodbye kiss for the road and before he knew it, he was well on his way back to his South Minneapolis neighborhood. The world looked so good to him, so fresh. The deep snowbanks that lined his route could not put a damper on his spirit, he was whistling a tune from long ago...and Brian NEVER whistled.

Is this love? He must have looked foolish to the guy sitting next to him at the stoplight. A crazy looking smile emanated from his face. He didn't care, the world was a wonderful place on this sunny afternoon.

No sooner had Brian opened the back door to his house than a car pulled up out front. He heard the auto stop, its brakes louder than normal, and he looked out the front window. *"Oh no...Annie!"*

Panic filled his mind. Did she know about him and Evelyn? He found himself checking his tie and hair, then realized that he hadn't changed out of his clothes from the night before. *"No! Gotta change! She'll know something is up!"*

Brian sprinted the steps upstairs two at a time and threw his coat, shirt, and pants into a pile on the floor as the doorbell rang below. Grabbing a t-shirt and baggy pants from a separate pile, he wildly re-dressed as he stumbled back down the stairs and toward the front door. *"This is going be the death of me!"* he muttered under his breath as he pulled the door open.

"Annie, what a pleasant surprise!" Konrad stammered, trying to catch both his breath and his wits. The beautiful red head held his newspaper up and chuckled.

"Sleeping in on a Sunday? What happened to the Brian I know? Did you kidnap him? Has he skipped town?" The bachelor blushed and returned a light laugh.

"What brings the beautiful Miss Annie to my humble abode on this blustery day?"

"Blustery?" she laughed louder, "You're certainly not a Minnesotan, are you? Will you be inviting me in or shall I stand here and freeze to death?" Embarrassed at his lack of manners, he sheepishly stepped back and allowed her to enter.

"So... to what do I owe the pleasure of this visit?" Annie turned to him and gave him the once over with her eyes.

"I just thought it would be nice to stop in and say hi. We hardly talk anymore and I kind of miss our conversations."

She looked at Brian for a moment and realized that she had probably overstepped her bounds. It was foolish for her to pine for him so badly that she would actually drop in unannounced, on a Sunday no less.

"I'm sorry that I stopped in before calling...how rude of me."

A smile crossed his unshaven face. "Don't worry about it Annie, you know you are always welcome here...anytime."

Brian really meant what he said, there was no denying the fact that she held a special place in his heart. Where that place was at the moment was quite concerning and puzzling, but he had very deep feelings for this woman. Annie snapped him out of a temporary trance, he was caught gazing at her beauty.

"You haven't read today's newspaper yet, have you? What am I saying... I am bringing your paper to you like a puppy."

"A loyal, devoted puppy." Brian countered with a smile. A cloud of guilt descended on his spirit. *She's loyal as can be...I am not.* Shame boiled up in him, but Annie diffused it with a quick statement that brought him back to earth.

"Did you hear about the Rosenbergs? How tragic! The feds think they are both spies for the Soviets! I can't believe it, how could they be so stupid, so disloyal, unpatriotic, especially in these times? It's absolutely unbelievable! They're going to get a long prison term, maybe even the chair! What is it that has gotten them in so much trouble?"

Brian's mind raced at this news. He had been following these events closely, with an abject paranoia, and now things were really hitting the front pages. Could he be in more danger than he realized?

"Honey, are you listening to me? I asked you, what do YOU think?"

Konrad took a moment to clear his mind and formulate a safe answer. He looked away from her and shifted his weight from one leg to another as his hands went to his head and his fingers worked their way through his disheveled hair. He was caught in a moment of annoyance as well as paranoia, he had to tread carefully so as to not give away his situation. It was this ruse that made him feel even more deceitful in regard to the woman he loved. He felt he could trust her, but worried that she would lose all respect for him, or worse yet, leave him.

"Jeepers, Annie, I don't know. We are living in crazy times. The government seems to be going out and looking for trouble, almost like the Salem witch hunts all over again. Anyone could be suspected nowadays, nobody is safe. Julius Rosenberg's brother in law was sending him all kinds of nuclear secrets from somewhere in New Mexico. Rosenberg and his wife would then send the stuff to Soviet spies somewhere. Her brother supposedly turned on them, gave information to the FBI in return for lesser charges. Espionage, plain and simple."

Annie paused a moment and processed what she had heard. "They seem so harmless. Do you think those two could really be guilty of espionage?"

Brian almost whispered his reply as an eerie tension suddenly grabbed hold of both of them.

"Anything is possible…anyone is possible. I would hate to think of what would happen in our art community if people started pointing fingers and making accusations. It could set our museum and the art crowd back ten years or more. Our funding could dry up and exhibits would cease. I hate to scare you, Annie, but we are living in strange times."

With this dark realization, Brian forced the topics to small talk on items of the day. Caught up in a sudden boredom and guilt at her unannounced drop in, Annie excused herself and left in a state of confusion.

Brian sure seemed strange… from the moment I first arrived. I wonder what is going on. He seems to be on edge, he must be hiding something.

The young woman pulled away from the curb and headed back to her apartment near downtown. She had no idea of the magnitude of the situation that her boyfriend was a part of. In fact, Annie had no idea of the degree of her relationship with Brian. To make matters even more complicated, Brian had no idea of their relationship either. Troubled times indeed.

****

Nineteen Fifty-One rang in with the same lack of clarity that Nineteen Fifty held and Brian had decided that he would buckle down and work harder at the museum. The best way to dodge the relationship conundrum with Annie and Evie would be to immerse himself in the newest exhibits and the business that was increasing from the east coast.

The young curator had pieced together much more information about the business than he was given by his superior as he now understood that the microfiche coming from the west was actually from the famed atomic research facility at Los Alamos, New Mexico. Denver, for reasons unknown to him, had become more of a risk and so the newest shipments back and forth were now coming out of the smaller airport at Dallas. The regional museum in Minneapolis was quickly growing in size and the different articles that were passed back and forth were passing through security without notice.

Brian had also gotten to know the curator in Dallas, Dr. Paul Reed, from his internship in New York. Reed was a smallish figure with about ten years of age on Brian, but what he lacked in physical size he made up for with tremendous intelligence and a fiery temper. Konrad had taken a liking to him from the first time they had met. Now the friends were on the inside of the business and both were very loyal to Dr. Brooks and the cause.

The shipments that had been occurring once or twice a month had now become weekly and money was passing through the Minnesota Museum of Art as fast as artifacts and film. Brian was now charged with directing the different contraband to their final destinations, in many cases he was typing up notes taken from Los Alamos and sending the finished manuscript on to the east.

Summit 1869, a.k.a. Summers, was also busier than normal. He had established a connection with a foreman inside the Honeywell manufacturing plant on the north side of town and was smuggling important documents as well. Aside from a booming business in home thermostat and heating devices for the average American home, Honeywell was one of the top defense contractors for the United States government and they were charged with building guidance and detonation devices for the military's nuclear missile program.

Nuclear bombs were used with maximum effectiveness on the Japanese in the summer of 1945 and newfound technology now made those obsolete. Bigger, more destructive bombs had taken their place and the government was toying with rocketry. A large rocket could deliver a payload anywhere in the hemisphere and would allow attacks and defense without the use of an airplane and crew. Rumor was that Honeywell was playing a major part in this plan, along with the U.S. Army's defense plant in Arden Hills, also north of the cities.

Summer's signals now appeared on the park bench two or three times a week and both men took to meeting in Brian 's office after the museum's operating hours. Despite the fact that the U.S. government was working harder than ever to get rid of Soviet spies and that the Rosenberg situation was dominating the news, it seemed that the covert traffic was more frequent than ever before inside the MMA.

Konrad was careful not to bring attention upon himself, but he was also working harder and was more loyal to the cause than ever before. Crated exhibits would arrive, the young curator would send them on for delivery to the west, and they would return from Dallas with important information enclosed. Then the items would be shipped with documents, microfiche, film, or American currency to the Soviet Bloc. West Germany and Finland would receive the western packages and would then smuggle them into either East Germany or the Soviet Union. It seemed too simple to be successful!

Dr. Brooks had also kept in touch with Konrad more frequently. In coded language, he conveyed the fact that the Soviets were catching up in regard to nuclear capability. He believed that the Rosenberg situation had not helped the east very much, but the work they were doing was bridging the gap and, as of the spring, the U.S.S.R. was right on the heels of the United States. Estimates were that the next six months of material shipped could put both countries at equal nuclear capability.

In Brian's mind this was perfect; there was nothing better to deter the use of nuclear weapons than a standoff between two major countries that had the same capability. They would effectively force a check on each other thereby eliminating the actual use of the weapons. Nuclear deterrence at its best...keep both sides scared of dying and they would not start the fight. The more weapons of equal power, the less they would be apt to use them. Both economies would grow as well because each country had to employ people and buy the materials to make the bombs. Everybody would come out winners. *Of course, if all goes wrong everyone will be dead."*

A very frigid January gave birth to an equally icy February and Brian found himself missing Evie. It seemed that every time he would have a free evening or weekend, she would have something of major importance going on in her life. Suspicion started to creep into his mind.

Is she seeing someone else? Am I just a quick fling? A good time?

Aside from seeing Annie at work they had only gone out a couple of times to movies and dinner. During the day both were much too busy to socialize and Brian sensed that she was smart enough to figure everything out if she got too close. He worked very hard to resist the temptation to take the relationship to the next step. There would be no engagement rings in either of the women's futures regarding the young curator. The cause came first, love of one's country overrode love of a woman.

Chapter Eleven

"Jeezus, what have I gotten myself into here?" - Jay Hoffman

William Alford arrived to work ten minutes late on Friday morning, this was a habit he couldn't ever seem to break. The stop at the bakery down the street always took up the extra ten minutes and by the time the coffee and pastries were consumed he found himself huffing his way up the steps of the Federal building.

Will was on the downside hill of fifty, less than five years to retirement if he could convince his wife that his pension would be adequate. Characteristically bald with a larger than healthy gut, he did his best to try and stay fit but the donuts and coffee spoiled his best efforts.

Alford started his career in law enforcement after a stint as a student at the University of Minnesota. Four years turned out to be two too many for him academically, after a training stop in St. Cloud for law enforcement, he joined the police force in South St. Paul.

Will liked working with people and had a difficult time coping with strikers at the huge meatpacking plants in the city. He felt a sympathy for the working man and had a philosophical problem with trying to hold the strikers down. Locking up a man who was trying to support a wife and kids on a paltry salary from the Armour or Swift meatpacking plants seemed less than fair, actually a crime in itself.

A devoted law man, he did his time on the force and then when the opportunity presented itself, he transferred to the Federal level in St. Paul. His record as an officer was stellar, he had no problem being accepted into the program and he flourished at this level. Aside from a stint as a military policeman at Fort Snelling during World War II, he was moved to the Minneapolis office to track international crime and war subversives.

The war ended with promotions granted for his strong efforts in keeping the cities safe and he was granted chief detective status in the international division. An honorable career was coming to a close for a man of great integrity and Will Alford was looking forward to retirement.

"ALICE! What is this pile of garbage doing on my desk! I told you, no new stuff on Fridays! How am I supposed to relax for the weekend?" His voice boomed across the floor; the junior detectives near his office made sure to stay away from the wrath of the boss. Alice, his secretary, was not fazed in the least. A small but sassy lady who could bring a bad attitude, Alice was not intimidated and Will knew it.

"You're not SUPPOSED to relax when you're at WORK!" she retorted. The junior officers were just as scared of her as they were of Alford, maybe even a little more. "That GARBAGE on your desk has to be taken care of if we are to keep America safe!" she bellered even louder. The young men on the floor cowered and pretended to be busy as Will settled into his desk chair and opened the first file.

"*Department billing...this shit can wait.*" He chucked the file onto the back credenza with a thud. "*Last week's performance report...we didn't do much, there wasn't a damn thing to do.*" This file followed the first one with another thud.

"*Hmmm...what's this? New York to Albuquerque? Santa Fe, Dallas, Midwest?*" A series of notes had been typed up in no particular form, some relating to the Rosenberg situation, others related to missing materials.

One note in particular described a package that was postmarked from Minneapolis to New York in December. Inside the package there had been a small painting with a suspicious letter and a large amount of U.S. currency buried at the bottom. This piqued Will's curiosity.

"Minneapolis, huh? That's weird. Currency from here? It doesn't make sense…would the Minneapolis Federal Reserve Bank be involved? Why us?"

There was something unique about this file but he couldn't put a finger on what it was. He would choose to handle this one himself, or maybe get a hand from one of the senior members on the floor.

The trouble was, the senior members of his staff were not very motivated. They were just putting in their time and to make matters worse, they would want all the credit if something big broke. Alford was the boss, but he didn't want to have to get into a pissing match over who would get the glory if something newsworthy came along. He would need to find a rookie with a solid work ethic and a respect for the senior officer.

"Alice, can you come in here for a minute?" Alice stopped typing up a report and slowly rose from her desk. The twenty foot walk seemed to take forever, but Alford wasn't about to ruffle her feathers, she was beyond loyal to him and above the highest value. He knew he could count on her if the going got rough and there were very few people he ever really counted on over the course of his life.

Alice shuffled to the door and he asked her to close it behind her. She settled into a chair and asked, *"What's up Chief?"*

'Chief' was her affectionate term for him, he had gotten used to it over the five years that they worked together and now he was quite fond of it. A gentle smile broke over his face as he asked his important question.

"If you needed to count on one rookie out there on the floor to break the biggest case of your life, who would you choose?" Alford paused and let the silence sink in. The ceiling fan slowly whirled above their heads. Alice turned and looked out on the floor at the filled desks.

"Thompson is a little snitch...always trying to get ahead on somebody else's work. Bradley is a smart kid, but he's so green. He'll be the one to accidentally shoot himself in the foot on the job." They both got a chuckle from that comment.

"Not much to choose from out there, huh?" the boss growled, not happy with any of the candidates.

"You know Chief, the Hoffman kid in the back over there is pretty sharp. He stays late, is polite, and he's had a little bit of success over the past couple of months. He helped break that shoplifting ring downtown, the one where they were stealing all those furs and sending them to Europe somewhere, remember?"

The big man sat up straighter and nodded. "Yeah. That was THAT kid?" Alford replied with interest.

She smiled and nodded with confidence, happy to assist her boss.

"Can you have him come in? And Alice... thank you."

He said the last phrase with genuine sincerity. Alice nodded with an even brighter smile and walked across the large workroom to Jason Hoffman's desk. Will could see her talking to him and he looked up with a bit of surprise at the big man's office. His head dropped suddenly and he rose from his chair looking like a kid about to be disciplined by the school principal.

"Sir, you wanted to see me?" the young officer inquired with quiet respect.

"Yes, Jason! Come on in." Alford replied, trying to break the ice and put the youngster at ease. "Have a seat."

Hoffman sat down and carefully studied the veteran's face and posture. Alford's years were starting to really show on him, he had always had a baby face but now the wrinkles were making an appearance on his light complexion.

"I have been looking over your work reports and quite frankly, they are impressive. I am looking for a partner on what could be a very important case here in the cities. I would need a large commitment of time and energy on your part if you are interested in helping me. Confidentiality would be a must during the whole endeavor, I would need to know that I can trust you. This could be the biggest case to hit the cities in a long, long time and if you screw it up I will have your badge. Can I count on you as a partner for as long as this takes?"

The young officer felt the sweat starting on his brow and under his arms. *What in the hell kind of case could this be? Holy shit, he's threatening to take my badge if I screw it up. Jeezus, what have I gotten myself into here?*

"Yes sir, you can count on me." His brain was spinning out of control and his knees wobbled as he made his way out of the office an hour later with a better understanding of what he would be required to do.

****

Alford and Hoffman began the arduous task of assembling all the different notes and facts that had been stuffed in the manila folder. Long days made up the first week of their work together and it didn't take long for Will to realize that the young detective he had picked was very sharp. Backtracking the postal system was not easy despite the mail stamps and postal tags on the items recovered. Some of this work had been already completed, but a majority of the material that had been enclosed was just thrown together.

A few things that were included didn't even seem to belong in the file. The older detective would ask the questions due to his many years of experience in crime and the young detective would answer with his extreme intellect and reasoning. They found that there was a productive chemistry building between them and things began to fall into place.

Why was there U.S. currency bound for New York? Why are the bills marked from the Philadelphia mint and not Minneapolis? Philly has a fed bank but we do too. The note makes no sense...is this some type of code? What is the connection to the Southwest? Rosenbergs? Los Alamos? Nuclear testing and development?

The two detectives slowly contacted people at the U.S. State Department, the Federal Bureau, and other insiders to get every scrap of information they could. People from all over the country were assisting them in putting a logical case together. The detectives found that for every failure or setback that they had there was two or three victories; this fed their work ethic and mission.

Over takeout food one evening during the second week of March, something suddenly struck the junior officer's mind.

"How come we seem to be the midpoint between New York and Los Alamos, New Mexico?" he blurted aloud to Alford between bites of chow mein.

Will stopped chewing for a moment and directed a quizzical glance at his partner. With a smart-ass tone, the older detective provided levity. "Well, you see when it comes to geography…"

Hoffman shook his head with frustration.

"They're not using our money, we have nothing of value to foreign powers here in the Midwest, but we are a logical halfway point for transit. We do have Honeywell over on the north side of town, the defense plant. Maybe we are the center point in the ring to move cash and goods out of our country. Think about it. Why would Minneapolis, Minnesota be so important? We actually have value here with defense contracts…we could easily intercept west to east goods, add some of our own, and send all the stuff to the coast where it gets sent overseas to a destination in the eastern hemisphere."

The downfall to experience is sometimes skepticism. A veteran with years of cases to his name sometimes sees so many of their theories disproven that they begin to ignore the obvious. Jay Hoffman didn't have this handicap yet; he was still for all practical purposes a rookie. His mind continued to grind out a possibility that seemed very real. The young detective continued to nod his head with thought as he consumed more of his meal. He felt he was right; the pieces of the puzzle were coming together for him.

"That's an awfully crazy stretch you are proposing in order to make this scenario work. You are assuming that someone is trying to spy for the Soviets. Maybe you are reading a little too much into this. A little too much Rosenbergs perhaps?"

The senior officer went back to his food, not really giving much credence to the theory.

"The real key to this thing is to either intercept some more stuff or break the code that the letter is written in." Alford said, suddenly serious.

The young detective fell silent for a while, his brain working again between bites. The more that the senior detective thought about it though, the more he thought that the kid might be onto something. *One more break. One more interception. Break that code.*

The problem was that there was no code to break. The letters were written very cordially in a friendly tone with topics that anyone would undertake on a normal conversation. The mentioning of the Rosenberg situation was more troubling; *How many people would bring up the Rosenbergs in their daily conversation?* The big break came at the end of the summer when postal inspectors at the airport in Bloomington found another package.

The cargo was supposed to go to the Museum of Modern Art in New York and a clumsy cargo handler accidently dumped it on the runway. The postal officials attempted to piece the package together and when they did about fifty thousand dollars in one hundred-dollar bills spilled onto the tarmac and started blowing away with the summer wind. Baggage men were chasing loose currency with a gusto, probably hoping to keep some for themselves. When all was said and done, most of the currency was put back into the package and delivered downtown to Alford and Hoffman.

Both men took their time to inspect the outer layer of the package carefully before opening it up.

"Look at the return address. Minnesota Museum of Art. Interesting...is this part of our case?" The senior detective took the lead with his thought out loud.

"I don't know... could be related." Jay Hoffman replied with an air of resignation; his ideas seemingly always criticized.

"What are the odds that we suddenly uncover a package that contains this amount of money in standard currency, one hundreds no less." Alford said. Both men shook their heads and looked from the parcel to each other. The older man spoke next with conviction.

"Let's open her up."

Carefully working the side of the box open with a scissors, it took less than a minute to pull out all of the contents. A friendly note from K to ABE along with a small glazed vase. Money was inside the vase as well as around it for padding.

Both men looked at the artwork and then at each other. "I think we should pay the museum a little visit." Alford exclaimed with a sly smile.

Chapter Twelve

"Sometimes life is just too hard to figure out." - Kit

Annie stepped off the bus at the corner near the front of the museum, gazed across the park at the fallen leaves and golden hues, and shivered noticeably as the autumn wind brushed her pretty face. She slowly ascended the marble steps with something heavy on her mind. She couldn't shake the feeling that she knew something must be wrong.

Aside from a handful of dates and a weekend fling or two, she had spent a most of her summer away from Brian. He seemed strangely aloof as of late and had been travelling to New York and Dallas much more often.

Is there another woman? Somebody in New York or maybe Dallas? The thought had been tugging at her mind and her heart was heavy with the realization that Brian might not be her man.

The warmth of the museum and its familiar scent engulfed her as she entered the large, ornate glass door and she smiled as she suddenly felt like she was at home. This place had become her refuge, she was spending most of her waking hours at work.

The tours picked up in frequency as schools were open again and teachers scheduled field trips for their classes. Daily chores consumed the rest of her working hours and by the end of each day Annie was ready to commute home to a hot meal and a warm bed. As tired as she was every day, Annie felt satisfied with her career and now only longed for a wedding ring from her elusive boss.

Trekking to her newly acquired office, she stopped in the workroom and picked up her mail from the familiar wooden box with her name on the front. She pulled Brian's mail and delivered it to his small, empty office. Placing the pile on the only open area of his desk, she looked around and noticed just now unkempt everything was.

"Poor man, he needs a good woman to organize his life." Moving a few knick-knacks and mementos into place on the wall shelves, she progressed to organizing piles of paperwork on his desk.

Straightening the lamp upon the desktop, she picked up a small note dated a month earlier. Feeling a moment of guilt over breaking confidentiality, the sensation passed as she read the note.

B,

Need to see you as soon as possible, things are happening. Come direct, the usual place. Ticket enclosed, same room. Hope all is well in your corner of the world.
AB

Annie's heart sank as she slowly lowered the note back onto the desk. Guilt over reading the note returned, her face now flush with a combination of embarrassment and surprise. She slowly stood up and moved out of the office, feeling suddenly numb and light-headed.

"Annie, are you ok?" her friend Kit asked softly.

"Uh, yeah Kit, I'm ok." Annie stammered, lost in thought at her desk. Their eyes met for a moment and Kit knew that the answer was false, something was definitely wrong.

"If you need to talk, I am here for you...you know that, right?" Annie nodded, still obviously disoriented. *Must be problems with Brian...hmmm.*

Kit felt sad for her friend but also secretly thrilled at the idea that the young curator might be back on the market. Carrying her own flame for Brian, she would start a fling with him the first chance she could get. The prospect of marrying him was as strong in her mind as it was in Annie's; she would keep this secret for fear of messing up her work and friendship.

If things change and the opportunity presents itself…all is fair after all. Kit couldn't contain her smile as she spun from Annie's office and headed down the marble hall.

Annie picked up the morning news and turned to the socialite section of the newspaper. Already feeling ill, her heart broke as she spied the picture on the front page and quietly read the caption below it.

"The beautiful heiress and her curator date attended the fall extravaganza in Minnetonka this weekend. A wonderful time was had by all."

Above the caption was a picture of Brian with Evie, drinks in hand, standing on a veranda. Both were smiling at each other and were dressed to impress; her man and the heiress made a striking couple.

"So, this is what is going on…" Tears welled up in her eyes as the realization of another woman was suddenly true. Dropping the open paper on her desk, she broke down crying as a feeling of foolishness passed through her.

The door to the office remained shut for most of the morning. Aside from one school tour, her Monday was thankfully slow. Annie struggled to compose herself and she could not go near Brian. There was no doubt in her mind that she would fall apart in front of him. As the day progressed, her sorrow turned to anger.

How could I be so stupid...so naive. What could he possibly see in me when he could have the richest woman in the Midwest? How could he do this to me? How dare he use me! By the time Brian approached in the late afternoon, she was ready to tear him apart.

"Hey Beautiful, haven't seen you around today?" The boss peeked into the office with a smile on his face.

"Don't beautiful me, you two timing slime!" she retorted, picking up the Swingline stapler off her desk. Brian ducked his head back from the door as the heavy steel office tool whizzed past, bouncing out into the hallway. Heads turned at the sudden commotion as the object clanked to a stop twenty feet away. Puzzled, Brian cautiously snuck his head back into the doorway.

"How could you! How could you?" she cried as she slumped back in her chair, totally dejected. Holding it together was not an option at this point. Brian slowly entered the room and moved to hug her.

"GET AWAY FROM ME!" she sobbed, as she pushed him back.

"She knows. She must have figured it out. She KNOWS!" Brian's stomach dropped as a feeling of doom engulfed him. He carefully settled into the chair across from her after quietly shutting the door.

"Annie, what's wrong?" he questioned very softly.

Looking up with tearful eyes, she pushed the newspaper across the desk and said "This."

Brian looked down at the picture and suddenly felt great relief. *Oh my, Evie. Thank god!*

A small smile gently crossed his face as he whispered "Annie, it's not what you think. This is really nothing." "Nothing?" she retorted with quiet anger.

"Nothing, really, that's all you can say? Nothing? We barely see each other anymore. I thought we had something special...now I see this. How long has this been going on? Nothing? This looks like something..." she trailed off with more tears reappearing.

"Seriously Annie, this is not what it looks like. I go out with her on occasion but it is really nothing serious...she has money and connections that help us out. I am tied into a whole new community with all of these events. We REALLY benefit from this kind of business. Annie, look at me...she is not YOU...she never will be." The words just tumbled out from his lips.

At that moment, Brian made his choice between the two women...it wasn't planned but it was final. He looked across the desk and realized that he couldn't ever let her down like this. She was too special to give up. He moved around the desk and she stood up, her eyes meeting his. Any doubts and lack of trust disappeared when he held her in his embrace and kissed her soft lips. At that point what had happened would be fixed, her heart overruled her mind. *I will fight for him.*

Brian left the office with a sense of relief a couple of minutes later; a crowd had gathered silently to see what was going on. Kit watched from afar as well and when she saw Brian's smile, she knew her chances were over again. She turned away and went for a long walk around the second floor of the museum. "Sometimes *life is just too hard to figure out.*"

The crowd quickly made like it was busy and scattered under the gaze of the boss. He retreated to his office and settled heavily into his chair, the weight of the world suddenly on his mind again. The note next to his typewriter suddenly caught the corner of his gaze.

"What in the world is this doing out?" he pondered as he picked it up. *"From Abe...this is two months old. How in the hell did it get here?"*

His heart skipped a beat as he noticed the pile of mail on the corner of the desk. *No, Annie...did she see this?* The dread that filled his mind twenty minutes ago in Annie's office now returned as he sat speechless in his own enclave.

There is no way she can know ABE. The note looks innocent enough. What should I say if she asks about it?

Lying had become as natural as breathing, in fact Brian's life was shaping up to be one big lie. He would have to find a way to get out of this mess, to put Annie's mind at ease.

Over the next couple of weeks Brian and Annie saw a lot of each other, from dates to weekend getaways, they took their relationship to a whole new level. Konrad made sure to stay clear of Evie and he brushed off her advances and phone calls, preferring to devote his time and energy to Annie. The episode with the stapler was quickly forgotten by Brian and with time Annie began to trust him again. Evie was persistent though, this made things dicey for the young curator.

To make matters even more crazy, shipments were arriving once a week from Dallas and new plans for timing devices and detonators were being delivered by Mr. Summers. "Summit 1869" was becoming a regular customer of the museum and employees were beginning to get to know him. He was always cordial and the staff had now taken a liking to him. Summers could expect many friendly greetings and a fresh cup of coffee within minutes of entering the Minnesota Museum of Art. The valued associate of Brian's appreciated the special treatment and sometimes visited with no business in mind. *It is always good to be someone special.*

Chapter Thirteen

"...what the HELL am I supposed to SEE?" - Jay Hoffman

The detectives stopped three times in a week to visit the museum, hoping to catch an introduction to Mr. Brian Konrad. The trouble was that every time they stopped in the young curator was out on business. They were charmed at the help desk by Konrad's pretty assistant, but up to this point they had made very little progress.

To add to the problem both detectives were temporarily pulled onto another case involving a professor at the University of Minnesota who was suspected of covert actions and teachings against the United States of America. A group was forming on campus with political ties to possible U.S. Socialists and this was ruffling the feathers of the Federal Bureau. The Minneapolis agents found their October filled with trips to the St. Paul and Main campuses of the U.

A light snow was falling as both detectives made their way down the front steps of the Federal building and out to the sedan parked on the street. This was the kind of snow that really didn't stay around, but could be a major cause of fender benders throughout the metro area.

"I'm getting too old for this shit." Alford muttered as he led the junior detective to the curb. Despite his youth, Hoffman struggled to keep up due to the fear of sliding on his backside down the stairway.

"Retirement can be any day now, right?" the younger officer replied with a nervous smile, watching his foot placement on each step.

"Not if my wife and kids have anything to say...the bills just keep piling up." the older man growled through the visible gray cloud that his mouth and nose emitted.

The large automobile pulled away from the curb and merged into the bustle of downtown traffic with the senior cop behind the wheel. Alford drove like he owned the road and on more than one occasion the younger officer let out a nervous noise while pushing a hand out to brace himself against the dash.

The seatbelts were not used, in fact had never been used and were jammed somewhere down in the bench seat. The car was so large that it was thought that seatbelts were unnecessary, a false feeling of security that both men should have recognized after pulling numerous bodies out of smashed vehicles throughout their years of experience. These occasions had apparently no permanence on their minds and, despite the aggressive driving, the safety restraints would remain unused. As the museum came into view up ahead, the older officer started issuing a plan of attack.

"Let me do the talking, I want you to keep your eyes open. Look for people around us and how they react to us…maybe they are part of this and have something to hide. I will take care of introductions. Don't act like anything is out of the ordinary, just keep cool. Watch everyone."

Hoffman concentrated on his orders and wondered silently what he would be looking for. He knew he didn't want to be the one to talk, he was quiet by nature and feared he would say the wrong thing and screw up the investigation.

What are we investigating, anyway? A package with money could be anything. My ideas have mostly been rejected…what the HELL am I supposed to SEE?

Hoffman followed the older man up the front stairs and into the entryway of the museum. The door off to the right had Brian Konrad's name on it. After a brief introduction at the front desk, both men turned to the door and Alford planted a firm knock on the wooden frame.

"Yes, come in." the curator invited, preoccupied with writing a note on his calendar for the next week. As he rose, the door opened and the two agents entered with a greeting and a formal introduction.

Brian's heart skipped a beat and both detectives noticed a sudden but subtle look of consternation cross his face. It disappeared as quickly as it had shown up; Brian regained his composure in an instant and invited both men in.

"So, to what do I owe the pleasure of this visit, gentlemen? Is it time for the policeman's fundraiser again?" he offered with humor.

"No sir, we missed you on that one." the younger detective responded with a chuckle.

Alford shot the young man a deadly glance, putting him in his place, then turned to Brian with a sly smile.

"We're actually here on business, Mr. Konrad. You see we had this incident out at the airport a while ago where one of your shipments fell off a transport truck and opened up on the runway. We were a little alarmed when a large sum of money was discovered, we think we recovered it and it was sent on its way...no harm done."

Both detectives were watching Brian intensely, but there was no sign of anything unusual, the young curator was a very good actor. Alford continued casually.

"We wondered why such a large sum of money would be shipped to the east coast by a museum such as yours."

The old detective paused long to set a tone and read his subject. Brian leaned back in his chair slightly, unalarmed on the surface but panicked inside, and he offered a sincere explanation to his guests.

"I can see how you would question something as different as this, but we ship all kinds of content between museums all the time. Most of what we ship is in material form, exhibit pieces and such. Come with me and I'll show you what we do. Do you have a moment?"

The offer was made warmly and both detectives nodded and rose from their chairs. They exited Brian's office and headed for the loading platform and offices one floor down. Brian felt relief as they left the stuffy office, he could calm himself down as they took a walk.

"Annie," Brian called out across the atrium, "We will be going down to the dock, I'll be back in a little bit."

Both detectives checked the beautiful redhead out, the younger one's gaze lingered a little longer than normal on her inviting figure. Brian noticed the interest and smiled as he whispered "Looks nice, huh? She's my girlfriend."

The last words hung with a manly bravado in the air. "Whoa," Hoffman whispered back, "Nice."

Both men exchanged grins as the older detective moved on, looking over some of the pieces of the exhibits along the way. After a five-minute saunter, they arrived on the ground floor and entered the shipping area. Despite it being mid-morning in the middle of the week, it was strangely quiet.

"Gentlemen, this is where we ship from, everything comes in and out of here." The detectives were puzzled as to why this was such a big deal, why were they led here? "As you can see, we ship a wide variety of goods from coast to coast. We are the midpoint of the American art world, excluding Chicago of course." Both feds nodded as Brian continued with confidence.

"From time to time we will ship currency from one museum to another. It is typically frowned upon because of problems like the one you guys encountered, but sometimes the risk is necessary. Museums will take delivery of money in exchange for museum pieces."

Alford took this momentary pause in the conversation to ask a key question that had bothered him for some time. After glancing at Hoffman to ensure his attention, the older man cut the silence.

"Why don't you just use Western Union to send a money order?"

The silence was deafening. It felt like ten minutes when in reality it was only ten seconds. Brian's mind raced for a moment before he omitted his rehearsed response.

"Western Union is usually used, but sometimes it is more convenient to ship cash securely. Union costs money and to ship deposits like this is also risky. I have to send for a courier or run an employee across town to the bank, deposit the cash, then write the money order. It is just as time consuming on the other end of the transaction. Time is money in this business."

Satisfied with his answer, he diverted the detective's attention by turning to a shipping log written on the blackboard along one wall.

"As you can see, we move a lot of stuff in and out of here. We prepare numerous exhibits upstairs as well; many of our pieces are brought in from somewhere else. We move a ton of stuff."

Another uncomfortable period of silence followed. The young detective turned to the curator with curiosity and a touch of sarcasm.

"It seems to me, Mr. Konrad, that your system isn't very secure. We picked up piles of your money off the runway." Alford smiled slightly as he watched Konrad squirm a little after Hoffman's statement.

"Well, uh, yes, sometimes we have a problem… not often though, thank god!" Brian retorted with irritation.

Jay Hoffman had been given the directive to look for things 'out of the ordinary.' As he glanced quietly at the shipping log he noticed a familiar pattern to his mind.

"Denver to Minneapolis, Minneapolis to New York. New York to Minneapolis, Minneapolis to Denver."

The young detective resisted the urge to reach up and turn the page on the chart; he was pretty confident that he knew what the next pages would reveal.

"I knew it." he mused to himself, barely able to keep a smile from emerging.

Konrad desired to end the visit quickly, he felt himself sweating under his sport coat. Into the elevator and back up to the second floor; very little was said. The quiet was almost condemning in Brian's mind, but he couldn't think of much small talk to offer. The elevator opened up at the desired floor and the men exited into the hallway. Kit was walking toward them, her high heels clicking on the marble.

The young detective had been playing the pattern and scenario out in his mind on the way up. The sudden sound that pierced the quiet of the hallway diverted his attention. Hoffman turned and felt a jolt of interest hit his brain, he thought she was breathtaking.

"Hello, Mr. Konrad, is there anything you need?" she offered professionally. Her eyes met the young detective's gaze and she was infatuated as well.

She shot him a sexy smile and he stepped in front of Brian to introduce himself. Offering an outstretched hand, he met her acquaintance and she introduced herself. Both could not take their eyes off each other.

"Well, we must be moving on." Konrad directed with a smile as he glanced toward Alford. The senior detective's look was one of partial annoyance and partial curiosity.

"Uh, yes. Time to go, Detective Hoffman."

Hoffman stepped back sheepishly, knowing he was caught. Kit moved around the group with a smile, holding the young detective's gaze the whole time.

"My god, is he CUTE!" she purred to herself as she moved further down the exhibit hallway. Looking down at his feet, the young man stole one more peek as the group moved to the front entryway.

"Gentlemen, it's been a pleasure to visit with you but now I must return to a pile of work. We're changing exhibits for the Christmas season and I am absolutely swamped with details. Thank you for stopping in, if there is anything else I can do for you... feel free to stop in anytime."

The curator issued this goodbye with such sincerity that the two detectives almost believed it.

"Thank you for your time, Mr. Konrad. Good luck with your new exhibit. We will be keeping in touch." Alford responded in a professional, serious tone. Brian would find it very hard to fall asleep this evening, something was wrong and he felt it deep inside his mind.

"What in the HELL WAS THAT back there, huh rookie?" Alford chuckled, but was somewhat serious at the same time.

"Uh, I don't know. I was just thinking through the curator's operation." Jay answered with embarrassed deference.

"You were thinking about something, all right, and I don't think it had to do with our curator friend." The young man's face was flush with crimson. He said nothing, hoping the topic would change on the way to the car.

"Maybe keep the drool off your chin and your tongue inside your mouth next time." The young detective smiled sheepishly as the old cop laughed from his belly for all to hear.

Chapter Fourteen

"You will pay, You will PAY!" - Miss Evelyn

Evie was absolutely furious. This wasn't supposed to happen in her world! How dare anyone interfere with her plans, this was her life after all. Nineteen Fifty-Two was supposed to be her year! How anyone could mess up her life, her plans, was beyond her wildest imagination.

Evie gets what Evie wants, no exception ever. If charm can't ensure happiness, then money can and there is plenty of green to go around. No one gets in Evelyn's way, if they do they will pay a hefty price.

The hatred was building now as she tossed precious pieces of furnishing around the room...she was a small tornado going off in the Minnetonka mansion and the hired help knew to let her be.

What set her off on this first week of February was simple. She had read the Minneapolis Star newspaper. In particular, she read the socialite section that listed prominent events such as births, engagements, weddings, and deaths throughout the metro area. The picture of Brian Konrad with his fiancée, a Mary Ann something or another, rocked the very foundation on which she stood.

"How could he do this? She's beautiful... what in the world? Reject me for someone as common as her? She's a nobody! Who is she? How could he?"

Nausea took over and the tiny woman crumpled to the carpet in a flood of tears. Her wailing could be heard through most of the house, the hired help had learned to ignore her selfish tirades since she had moved in from out east. A spoiled little brat, they would exclaim quietly behind her back. If she overheard them, they would be fired in an instant. This was not just another fit from the overindulged heiress...this was something more serious.

The young socialite picked herself up in a fit of rage and began tossing things around the room again. Her anger built as she wondered how he could reject her in favor of someone else, someone so *common*. "You will pay! You will PAY!" she screamed as she tossed a lamp onto the floor, creating a wave of glass as it shattered and bounced wildly. "I will get you, Brian Konrad, if it's the VERY, LAST, THING I DO!"

****

Brian had indeed proposed to a surprised and thrilled Annie on New Year's Eve, technically New Year's Day of 1952 as the streamers flew and the noisemakers all sounded. He had planned this since Thanksgiving of the year before, and this event seemed the perfect moment to pledge his undying love to his bride to be. Annie was completely stunned, then giddy beyond any happiness she had ever experienced. Her dream, their dream, was coming true. She would be Mrs. Brian Konrad.

Kit was also at the New Year's party and had suspected something like this for some time. The devoted friend of the bride to be was genuinely happy for her, for Kit had started seeing a young detective from downtown. Jason Hoffman was at the party that evening in the museum as a guest of Kit. They were now an item as well.

The note was concealed in a shipment from New York that arrived on the first day of March. Brian had been expecting something sooner or later, but had seen nothing since before Christmas of the year before. Things were uncharacteristically slow and this was a source of worry for him. Summers had stopped coming around as well, so much that some of the workers in the museum were openly worrying about why he didn't visit anymore.

Konrad suspected that maybe something had gone awry, but he laid back quietly and enjoyed life with his new fiancée.

"Who knows, maybe this thing is over and I can go on with life normally. A great career with high status, the love of my life, what could go wrong?"

The young curator recovered the small package from the shipping crate and, after retiring to his secure office, he opened the note.

K,

> Return to NY immediately. Urgent. Usual arrangements made. By rail, tix waiting at Union, StP. Contact, set date, round trip, asap. Urgent. 1869 also. Contact.
> ABE

A shudder consumed Konrad despite the fact that the temperature in the office was at least 78 degrees.

"This looks bad. This looks really serious. Why travel by rail? Is Summers supposed to come with? I can't call ABE, shit, they'll pick the call off. It's way too dangerous. How do I contact Summers? He gave me directive NOT to call." Brian was confused and his mind was racing one hundred miles per hour.

"What about Annie? How in the world am I going to explain it to her? Sooner or later I have to explain it all. What will she say, or do? God help me I am in trouble!"

Konrad fell back into his chair, hyperventilating. Pulse racing, vision becoming blurred, he felt like he was having a heart attack. Brian willed himself to calm down, his brow was dripping with sweat and his hands were shaking.

"Good god, get a hold of yourself man. This is no big deal. I'll contact Summers in the morning. Annie can

cover the museum for a week or two, she's done it before. This is no big deal..."

Opening his desk drawer carefully, he reached in and grabbed a bottle of bourbon. He poured a double shot into his empty coffee cup and took a quick gulp. The warm wave hit him as he sat back in his office chair.

The young man calmed down considerably as he worked his way through the plan. It was indeed no big deal as he had been doing this for two years without a single problem. The detectives from downtown had not been around since before Thanksgiving, there was nothing to fear. *"Hell, Jason and Kit are even dating now!"*

While remaining ever cautious, Jason and Kit were now close friends of Annie and Brian. Konrad stopped by Annie's office and the two left for home and a cozy dinner on this cold, spring evening.

****

Jay and Kit were indeed friends; this made it all the more awkward when he decided to enlist her help in the case concerning Brian Konrad. He took his time to approach the situation in the proper manner. If Kit thought she was being used their relationship would be over and he was not ready for that possibility. In fact, Hoffman was pushing their romance in the other direction. He was more serious about their future than her and he came to the quick determination that she was 'the one'.

The opportunity presented itself at a quiet dinner downtown on a Saturday night. Kit looked stunning as usual and he recognized a lengthy lull in their conversation as they waited for their entrees.

"Say beautiful, we should really take some time to catch one of the latest exhibits downtown at MMA." Kit smiled at the compliment, not the suggestion.

"Why in the world would we want to go hang out at my work? I spend too much time there as it is."

"But you don't spend time there with me. I love spending time with you...even in a boring museum."

"Boring is right." Her hand moved across the tablecloth to lie upon his. "We have much better things we could be doing." The excitement flooded his demeanor and he almost lost track of his purpose.

"You know though, I do find your work much more fascinating than mine. You seem to be one of the few who really runs the show over there." The flattery was apparent on her expression as she laughed softly. Jay continued his pursuit.

"All the stuff that comes in and goes out of there...it's amazing how much art moves across this country. Where do you guys get it all from and where does it all go. Certainly, your museum can't hold it all."

Kit was enjoying the attention that her boyfriend was giving her, usually they tended to focus on his career and day more than hers.

"We do move a lot of goods. Our museum is quickly becoming one of the best in the country. It is an exciting time to be working with Brian and Annie. They make a cute couple, don't they?"

"Not as cute as us." Jay placed his hand on top of hers and caressed her lightly. After dinner was finished, he moved to the next step of his plan.

"You know Kit, we should make a day of touring the museum...maybe tomorrow afternoon? I would really like to see all the new stuff, even the behind the scenes stuff that only you could show me." Kit felt an air of importance with the last statement. "I think we can arrange a private tour."

Chapter Fifteen

" I ALWAYS get what I want!" - Miss Evelyn

Kit and Jay made their way downtown in the early afternoon; they had very little else to do on a lazy Sunday. Despite visitors mulling through the marble corridors and bright exhibit rooms, there seemed to be few employees on duty. Kit didn't need assistance, she took her boyfriend through most of the exhibits, sometimes stopping and admiring the period art pieces, other times moving quickly through the boring stuff.

"So… tell me, what happens behind the scenes?" Jay asked carefully after an hour of art inspection.

"What do you want to know?" Kit whispered with a smile, feeling suddenly naughty. Hoffman picked up on her inference right away and laughed quietly, his eyes meeting hers.

"We can't do that here!" he exclaimed privately with a blush coming to his face. "Why not?" his girlfriend countered with a giggle. "There's no one here!"

The offer was beyond tempting, but he had to keep his composure and focus. "Hey, can I see what's coming in? The latest stuff? Where its coming from and going to?"

Kit's excitement level dropped as she wondered why he didn't want to play. *Am I more boring to him than this artwork?* He read her mind and assured her with a gentle comment.

"We can play a little later. I'm just curious about stuff...this is a fun little adventure, isn't it?" The young woman's spirits lifted as she led him to the elevator and down to the loading dock.

After wandering for what seemed like an eternity, Hoffman made his way to the log book hanging on the wall. Kit perused the cartons and crates, noting out loud the destination and contents when they were revealed.

Page by page, the young detective's suspicions became a reality. There was a pattern and it was the same pattern he had noticed on his earlier visit. This wasn't one page though, it was almost all of them. He also took note of the frequency, size of parcel, and time of delivery and departure. Jay Hoffman would have killed for a camera and five minutes alone. He would have to rely on his memory.

****

Monday morning broke bright and cheery across the Midwest. Miss Evelyn woke up the same way she did every morning, assistants to wait patiently on her every wish. Applying her makeup ever so carefully, she dressed in the most revealing outfit she owned.

Donning an overcoat, she called for her chauffeur and in a matter of minutes was seated in the back of the limousine that was headed toward downtown Minneapolis. This matter had been brewing for weeks and now needed attention. It was time to fix the situation in her favor.

The large, dark auto pulled up directly in front of the stone façade of the museum. The driver moved around to the passenger side and opened the door for Miss Pomeroy. She gracefully slid out of the back of the car, aware of the gawking public who strained to see what important person was arriving in style. She always loved this part...people would stare in wonder and jealous amazement as she took her time to show off.

She was beautiful and she knew it. Up the steps she delicately climbed; if she could she would have had the chauffeur carry her as it would be much more like something royalty would experience. As it was, everyone took note of the regal Ms. Evelyn and that was the way it should be.

Brian had left Minneapolis for New York very early in the morning with Summers in tow, but Annie was on duty and was called to the front desk when Evie arrived. The two women recognized each other immediately and a tense moment of silence emerged.

"Is Brian here? I must see him at once." Evie demanded.

"Brian is out of town at the moment. Is there anything I can help you with?" Annie responded coldly.

"There may be. Is there a place we can talk? Privately?" Evie continued with a demanding tone. Annie glared at the visitor.

"Follow me."

Annie led the heiress to Brian's office and offered her a chair, closing the door behind them. "So, what can I do for you?" she began.

"You can start by leaving my man alone." Evie growled in a low voice.

Annie slowly fiddled with the engagement ring on her finger, making sure Evie had a good view of the treasure.

Seems to me that Brian is now MY man."

Evie glared across the table at her adversary, not willing to lose.

"You know he was seeing me while he was supposedly with you. We made wonderful, passionate love at my lake home. I can give him more than you ever will, in fact I already have." The hatred in each word was intended to set Annie off.

"Well, aren't you revealing. For someone so fortunate and put together, it is amazing to see how much of a poor loser you are. This game is already over. Brian chose me."

Evie was boiling inside, if there was anything she could throw at this moment it would have been sent sailing into Annie's face.

Annie sat back with a cold grin and flashed the gold ring again.

"You bitch. This isn't over, not even close to over. I will have him, not you. I ALWAYS get what I want." Evie retorted with pure evil in her tone.

"I'll make sure to send you an invitation to our big day. You can sit right up front." Annie countered with glee.

Evie stood up abruptly, turned toward the door, and let herself out with a slam. Her heels clicked madly all the way down the hall and out the atrium doors. Annie sat back, now noticeably shaking from the encounter.

"Will she really try to steal Brian? Of course she will, the little bitch gets everything she wants. Not this time."

Annie now realized that she needed a good, stiff drink to calm her senses. She walked down to the front door to make sure her adversary was gone and then retreated back to Brian's office, closed the door behind her, and reached into his bottom desk drawer.

Pouring three fingers worth of bourbon into her man's empty coffee mug, she leaned back in his chair and sipped away. Within minutes her nerves were back to normal and she felt all warm and cozy. "Take my man...that is NOT going to happen."

Chapter Sixteen

"I KNOW EVERYTHING!" - ABE

Brian was well past Cleveland on the express to New York. Seated next to him was Summit 1869, also known as Mr. Summers. Both men said little in order to cover their relationship, most of the trip was nothing but aimless small talk. There were moments during the ride where there was enough privacy to speculate at why they were being summoned, by train no less. Neither passenger had a clue as to any of what was happening and it was clear that whatever was going on was urgent.

Their train pulled into Grand Central station late on the next day and there was a ride waiting at the curb for them. The driver held up a sign and within a minute they were on their way uptown to the Waldorf. After dropping their luggage in separate rooms and admiring the view and accommodations, both men returned to the sedan waiting at the front door.

The duo made their way to the same building that Brian had visited on his previous trip. The route, pattern, and movements had not changed. Everything about the visit was choreographed, right down to the minute. Nothing could be held to chance when it came to security; the U.S. government could shut the whole program down in a moment had they ever cracked the case or figured what this huge building in the center of Manhattan really was. Konrad entered the same room at the end of the hallway and found Dr. Brooks seated in his usual chair.

"Gentlemen, so good to see you!" the old man called loudly from the far end of the room. "It's been too long!"

Dr. Andrew Brooks smiled that confident smile that he always seemed to muster up, even in times of trouble. Brian suspected it was great acting, but he enjoyed the old man's company just the same, regardless of the circumstances.

"Please grab a place to sit. Norman, get these men something to drink!" The butler at the sidebar now moved quickly to fill the orders of the two guests. With drinks delivered, ABE began his assessment of the situation they faced.

"First of all, I understand congratulations are in order for Brian! You have found yourself a bride...congratulations indeed." Brian wondered how the old man knew, after turning to look at his colleague the answer was evident. Summers turned away slightly, betraying his guilt.

"Oh, come on now, you didn't think I wouldn't know. Don't blame Summers, he's just being loyal. I KNOW EVERYTHING!" Brian looked at the old man. He seemed to be aging quicker than normal these days but there was still an eerie look that spoke of incredible danger and violence.

The old man's expression turned dark quickly; his tone changed for the worse.

"DAMN IT, how could you let this happen. You know the rules, no ties to the outside. Did you not understand me?!" He was screaming now and the young curator was all the way back in his chair, visibly frightened. "HOW?!"

With that final exclamation, the old man sent his drink flying toward the wall and it shattered and sprayed debris everywhere. Both of the guests were now frightened and were breathing with difficulty.

"You WILL end this relationship...this, this, situation! There is no question, this is final! Do you UNDERSTAND me?"

Neither guest could say a word. Both men knew that Dr. Brooks could have them terminated with a single order. This was real, it was scary, and both men were frightened for their lives.

"Yes sir." Brian mumbled very weakly. "I will take care of this."

The old man had a succinct way of striking the utmost terror into his subjects. He held his eyes wide open, locked on Brian, seemingly less than a foot away...too close for comfort. The silence in the room was deafening. After what seemed like an eternity, Brooks moved back to his chair and sat down with an air of total control.

"Very well then, onto bigger things." the leader continued in a less caustic tone.

"Our business has slowed down significantly, as I am sure you have noticed. The feds are now onto us pretty good. You guys are safe for the most part in Minneapolis, but out here they are making great gains. Philadelphia is now out of the loop, Denver as well. We risk a lot by continuing in Dallas, but still need that connection. The Rosenbergs have pretty much burned us at Los Alamos, there is nothing coming from there anymore. That is why you guys are so slow now."

Turning with confidence to the other man, Dr. Brooks continued.

"We still have Honeywell, so make sure you protect that. Right Summers?" Konrad's partner nodded slowly and responded timidly.

"That shouldn't be a problem sir. We still have the defense plant in the Twin Cities too."

Brian listened intently, learning more about their operation.

"Very well then. There will be some changes. Keep your guard up. Our plans are still working, but there will be a few new things in the works. The money is very good."

With that statement, a gentleman emerged from a side door carrying two briefcases. He placed one at each of the guests' feet and left the room by a different door. Dr. Brooks looked at the two men with a gentle grin and newfound excitement.

"Well? Go ahead and open them!" he ordered as his smile grew wide.

Brian lifted the case to the walnut coffee table in front of him and Summer did the same. The metal, spring loaded clasps snapped free and the men opened the cases; inside were bundles of one hundred dollar bills. Konrad's eyes bugged out at the realization of what he was holding. There must have been one hundred thousand dollars in the case, all of it his.

****

Brian's temper very rarely got the best of him but now he was about to go off. Summers turned, almost sheepishly toward Konrad.

"I'm sorry Kon, I had no idea he would freak out...he just asked me and I told him...I didn't know."

Brian pointed to the driver and then to his ear. The chauffeur would tell the old man everything; for all they knew the car was bugged. He glared at Summers and then focused back out the window into the rain and Central Park. The limo came to a stop and both men lugged their full briefcases into the hotel.

"Look, I know you didn't know and you were being loyal to the old man, but come on...you told him about me and Annie?!"

Exasperation filled his voice. He was tired and emotionally worn out despite the fact that he was suddenly much richer. Brian couldn't think of anything else to say; he just looked at his partner and shook his head from side to side as Summers expression dropped and he looked away.

Both men retired to their elegant rooms and Brian found himself looking out on the magnificent expanse that was Central Park. The rain had subsided now and night was falling...New York was always fascinating at night. His mind wandered to

Annie and he missed her. It was time for a new plan, there was no way he was going to call everything off.

He reached for the phone on the nightstand and within a minute or two was connected to Minneapolis and the love of his life.

"Hey Beautiful, how are things in small town America?" Annie giggled back with happiness as she recognized his voice immediately.

"You will NEVER guess who paid me a visit at the museum today!"

"Umm, let me see, the President of the United States?" he playfully replied.

"Nope. Even better. Miss Evelyn Pomeroy."

There was a sudden silence as Brian's mind flipped in his skull.

"What?" he stammered.

"Yes, playboy. She was looking for YOU." Silence again.

"I told her you were gone. She said you two had the most intimate encounter in the history of man and woman." More silence, Brian's heart dropped along with his jaw.

"She says she's going to win you back. I told her off. She wasn't too particularly happy, especially as she kept staring at my engagement ring!"

There were very few times in Brian's life when he was truly speechless; this was one.

"Uh, Annie, you know I love you more than anything in the entire world, right?" he stammered quietly.

"Of course you do!" she blurted playfully. "You're not going back to her, are you?" She softly asked.

"I gave you the ring, not her. I would never go back to her, or to anyone else for that matter. You're are the woman that I have chosen to spend the rest of my life with, ok?"

He was as sincere as he had ever been in his life. Annie believed him in an instant.

"That's what I like to hear. Hurry back, I miss you and have a big surprise for you."

After a few more tender moments of conversation he signed off for the night. In forty-eight hours he would be back home to a much more comfortable reality; he couldn't wait to return.

Chapter Seventeen

"A nice wedding gift for my friend and his wonderful bride." - Summers

The trip back to the Midwest was as quiet as the trip out. Both men had patched up their situation and now seemed much closer. Summers didn't say much, but he really didn't have to. There was a certain loyalty there that Konrad felt, it was something that seemed to be missing in many of his past relationships. The curator felt that Summers could be trusted despite his small screw up.

The travelers parted ways at the Union Depot in St. Paul and Annie was waiting in her car to pick him up. They exchanged small talk on the way back to Brian's place and Annie had already planned to spend the night and make up on lost time. They spent the whole weekend together and somewhere in the midst of Sunday afternoon Annie began to tell Brian of her life with her ex-husband. She didn't really know why she chose to reveal so much of her past...perhaps it was because she and Brian became so close emotionally.

Annie had never been this close to anyone in her life, including her first husband. What was revealed actually caught Brian by surprise and made him angry in a number of ways. The abuse that Annie suffered at the hands of a bully who degraded all women made Konrad want to kill him immediately. The farmer from Central Minnesota had verbally abused and physically tortured her for the better part of five years until she was forced to run for her life. She never expected to survive.

The best part of the story was that she did survive. Annie rebuilt her life with very little support. She had no siblings and her parents went their separate ways when she was young. Her mother died of alcoholism when she was ten and her maternal grandparents raised her into her late teens.

A short stint at college brought her to the cities, but this reprise was short-lived as her grandmother then passed away. It was at this point that she met the charming farmer from outside the rural town of Albany who promised her a safe and secure life. With her grandfather in a rest home, this arrangement seemed like the best thing she could ever hope for.

Everything changed after the wedding vows and she found herself a slave to a man she now realized she barely knew. Physical torture, emotional torment, and rape followed as she struggled to maintain her sanity and life.

After one particularly brutal beating she fled to a friends' house in the cities and promised to never return. Annie hired a cheap lawyer downtown and a divorce settlement and decree were drafted. Roy, her abusive husband, never contested the situation and chose instead to pursue his next victim in the bars around the rural farm communities of Albany, Avon, and St. Joseph.

The story made Brian's blood boil and for some strange curiosity he had a desire to pay Roy a visit. The opportunity presented itself a month later when early one evening the young man hopped in his sedan and decided to take a drive north. As the city turned gradually to rural countryside the traveler kept asking himself why he was making the potentially dangerous trek.

"What in the hell am I doing? I should just let sleeping dogs lie...this could be really bad."

Despite all efforts to talk himself out of the drive, he pushed on through the early evening. The light of a long day was slowly drifting to the blues and grays that made one's eyes more tired than normal. Keeping the speed limit in mind, Brian found himself struggling to concentrate and keep his eyes on the road. His muttering to himself was the only thing audible over the drone of the engine and whine of the tires on the asphalt roadway and it barely kept him awake.

After two hours on the road Brian pulled up to the local watering hole in the small farm town. He walked into a darkened little dump of an establishment with a bartender who looked to be ten minutes away from death.

The blue tinted air gave off a putrid scent that burned the nostrils. Despite being a smoker himself, Brian had all he could do to tolerate the nasty interior of Albert's Roadhouse Bar. Hoping to become accustomed to the surroundings, he carefully made his way toward the man behind the bar.

"Hi, how are you doing?" The politician in Brian came out despite his less than enthusiastic greeting. "Can you tell me where Roy Olson's place is?"

The bartender gave him the once-over with his lazy eyes and asked "Why you want to know?"

The city-slicker looked away for a moment, surveying the situation, wondering if Roy was in the bar, and then responded with quiet confidence.

"I heard he was living in these parts. I'm an old friend of his family...was wondering how he is doing? Just passing through and thought I'd say hi." The man behind the bar looked at him with suspicion, but complied with a location.

"He lives out north of here about two miles. Name's on the box out front. His place is on this street here, it'll be on the left side of the road...a big, white barn to the right of the house...across the driveway."

The out of towner took a momentary pause to calculate and memorize the directions he was given; the silence between the two men was uncomfortable despite the noises of the droning jukebox and clicking of the far-off billiard balls.

"You crazy or somethin'?" the old man questioned with a wild look. "Do you know who you are looking for?"

Another pause followed as Brian shrugged in response, puzzled now with the bartender. The questioner had a look of astonishment as he continued his line of reason. He looked up, across the bar to make sure no one was paying any attention, then proceeded.

"Roy Olson is one bad ass of a man. I don't care who you say you are, you don't want to mess with him. He will kill you as sure as I am standing here in front of you. Even the sheriff is afraid of him....one bad ass of a man."

Konrad was now rethinking his visit with Annie's ex-husband as it was quickly becoming a bad idea. His nerves overcame him and forced him to a hasty goodbye and a fast exit. His senses relaxed after he sat down in his sedan and took in a few breaths of cool air. The fresh country smell and chirping of cicadas helped lower his pulse and encouraged him to continue on his quest. *"What the hell.... I have come this far."*

Brian started the vehicle, turned in the gravel lot, and hurried on his way; the summer sun of June was just about gone and he knew he would need any remaining daylight to locate the right farm. At almost exactly two miles he spotted the black mailbox with 'Olson' poorly scribbled in white paint on the side.

The nervous curator pulled into the dusty driveway, parked on the side, and after quietly shutting the driver's door sauntered up to the house. *"This is crazy...what the hell am I going to say to this guy?"*

He knocked on the door and there was no answer. It wasn't quite dark enough for lights to be on inside but a noise from the barn forced him to turn and approach the large structure. As he entered the building, his nostrils picked up the sharp scent of dairy cows. Taking care not to step in a mess, the city slicker moved toward the lineup of animals.

"Roy Olson? Are you here?" Brian yelled over a noisy machine.

"Yeah. Here in the back. Who's wants to know?" The voice was low and burly, the growling sound of a big man. Brian questioned his decision to make the trip again as he moved down the row of milk cows to the back.

A large man was hammering away on a machine that didn't want to seem to comply with his wishes. Filth and stench seemed to hover over him. A low, continuous chorus of swear words were being emitted and the man turned to face Brian, shutting down the noise.

"What do you want?" he inquired with callous caution. He didn't know the stranger in front of him and didn't have the time for small talk.

"My name is Brian Konrad. I'm from the cities. I am marrying your ex-wife." He paused, gauging the reaction from the large farmer.

"What the hell do you want from me? Money? Ain't got none. Sympathy? Got plenty for you, she's a nasty woman. What do YOU WANT?" Anger was rising in his voice.

"Just wanted to meet you, to see if you were everything she described. You are." With that, Brian turned and quickly left the building with a combination of fear and loathing building up inside of him. In no time at all he was pulling out of the driveway and heading for home. Brian Konrad's mind went numb.

A dark sedan pulled away from the driveway to the east and moved into the Olson's driveway.

Summer insects were chirping away along with a few birds as the night was now falling in the country. There was noise coming from the barn, the same barn that Konrad had just left. The man entered the building amidst the noise and looked around; he had been in a few of these workplaces in his lifetime.

A familiarity led him to the back of the building where Roy Olson was again pounding away on a machine.

"Hey you, asshole!" the man yelled, drawing the farmer's attention and making him turn around to face the intruder. The farmer was down on his knees and spun to find a boot connecting with the side of his head. The big man fell to the floor unconscious.

The intruder walked to the far wall and grabbed a long, thick rope from a hook. He returned and grabbed a couple of pieces of bailing twine from the top of the machine and tied the big man's arms and legs securely.

Next was the noose. He worked the rope expertly and in a matter of a minute had the rope hung over a rafter beam and secured on a large animal in its stall. The large loop went around the farmers' neck as he was propped up against the wall. A couple of slaps awakened the dazed farmer; he was immobile.

"You're the piece of shit who beat Annie almost to death, huh? How does it feel to be the victim? Not so tough now, are you, you sonovabitch!"

The farmer moaned, not quite aware of the situation and his imminent end. His eyes widened as the realization of what was about to happen came upon him and he started to plead for his life.

"Shut the hell up, asshole, you're too late! This is for Annie and Brian!"

The intruder walked over to the cow with the rope around its neck and he led the animal up the walkway. The struggling farmer flailed away as he was lifted up off his feet and up to the rafters. In a matter of minutes the death struggle was over; the farmer was gone.

The man lowered him, cut the rope in a frayed fashion with a machete hanging on the wall, fastened the end from the animal to a post, and kicked a bucket over near the corpse.

"Serves you right, you rotten sonovabitch." he muttered one last time as he walked out of the barn. Summers drove all the way back to the cities with a crazy grin on his face. *A nice wedding gift for my friend and his wonderful bride.*

Chapter Eighteen

"...those farm hicks up there would probably elect me as
their mayor!" - Summers

Brian Konrad felt a sudden panic overtake his
mind as his future bride showed him a note from a
friend in Albany, Minnesota.

"My ex is dead...hung himself in the barn, go
figure. I'm not even sad. He deserved it." Annie
stated this in a low, cold voice that was barely
audible.

"When did that happen?" Brian responded as he
brought her into an embrace.

"It's really not a big deal. Sometime last week."
she whispered as she pulled away.

"You used to love him, once upon a time. I can
understand if you are sad." She pulled away from
him with a little bit of force.

"I will never be sad for that man and what he put me through. Good riddance."

Brian wondered if there was more to the story. *"Would the police start to question people in town about a stranger moving through? What about the bartender who gave him directions?"*

Luckily no one really gave a damn about the cranky farmer who made more enemies than friends. The bartender was smart enough to tell no one anything; it was one less troublemaker in his establishment on a Friday night, someone he would not miss.

The signal was on the trashcan across the street, Brian could see it from the front steps of the museum. Summers would be stopping by on business sometime after nine o'clock in the evening. Brian always wondered what was next, what would need to be moved to the coast and this time was no different.

Staying late and sending Annie home, Brian waited on the front steps of the MMA as the sun dropped in the west. The temperature remained over 90 for most of the day, but with the sunset and a breeze it was now a comfortable 78. As Summers crossed the park and climbed the steps Brian realized that he did not want to go in. For the sake of security, he knew it was much too dangerous to sit outside and so he reluctantly retreated with his guest to the small office.

After closing the door behind him, Summers started the conversation with a tidbit that startled Brian.

"Hey, did you hear about the farmer up north who hung himself in his barn? It was on 'CCO the other day." Summers smiled as he waited for the curator's response.

"Uh, yeah, he was my fiancée's ex." The older agent could not hold back his glee with his next exclamation.

"Well guess what, the sonovabitch had it coming to him." A bizarre look of amusement took over the older man's face.

"What do you mean?" Brian inquired, wondering why there was such a fascination with the event on the part of his colleague.

"You know, he pleaded and begged for his life. It was wonderful! He had his demise coming to him...totally deserved it. Annie would have loved it. Arms and legs flailing, eyes bugged out to here!" Summers was bragging about his accomplishment with a satisfied smile, hands out in front of his face and a crazed excitement in his eyes.

"What in the hell are you talking about?" the curator replied with sudden alarm.

"Here's the deal. I followed you up to Albany…I know, I know, I should have told you. But there was no way you would let me go with and I had to watch out for you. Who knows what that crazy bastard could have done to you? I waited across the road until you left and then I took him out, simple as that."

Satisfaction for a job well done oozed from every pore of his being. Brian was puzzled, he couldn't seem to grasp the situation. There were too many questions left unanswered in his mind.

"Why in the world would you kill Annie's ex-husband?" A momentary pause followed as Summers seemed to contemplate the question that was posed to him.

"Why, he hurt Annie, right?" was the simple response from a smiling but serious Summers.

"Wait, how do you know he hurt Annie?" Brian questioned with seriousness, not sure he wanted to know the answer.

"That is for me to know and for you to find out. I can't tell you without getting in big trouble." Konrad felt goosebumps forming on his skin as the dialogue took a creepy turn.

"Brooks has you following me, huh? Watching my every move?" Summers shifted his weight from one foot to another, the smile suddenly gone from his face.

"I wouldn't say following you. I'm not watching your every move, but I am keeping you safe and yes, Brooks has you under surveillance. I am supposed to let him know when you have broken off your relationship with Annie, but don't worry...I have already lied about that. Your relationship is safe with me."

Brian slowly dropped into his chair; his mind was racing and a growing rage toward Brooks was clouding his thinking.

"I'll be damned, he doesn't trust me." Brian stammered, "I should have guessed it would come down to this. The old man doesn't trust anybody."

Summers tilted his head a little and smiled faintly. "I wouldn't say he doesn't trust you...he just doesn't trust your judgement while you are involved with Annie. Truth be told, I wouldn't trust you either. She has you wrapped around her little finger."

Brian shifted in his chair, trying to take the situation in. "Wait a minute, how did you know about the farmer and Annie? Do you have my place bugged? Are you listening in on us?"

Summers lowered himself into the chair across from Konrad and softened his tone.

"No, I would never do that to you. When the old man found out about the both of you, he had a background check done on Annie. He actually sent someone up to Albany to investigate her. The abuse in that household was known all over town, everybody felt sympathy for Annie. The simple fact was that the people up there were all scared of Olson and his posse of friends. I have followed you from here to your house and anywhere in between on orders from the old man. When you headed up to central Minnesota, I pretty much knew what was going on. "

The older agent paused and raised his hands up in the air, giving off a nonchalant shrug as he continued. It was obvious that this was no big deal to the assassin.

"You left the farm and I figured I could settle a score for you and your bride. A wedding gift so to speak. You won't ever have to worry about him again." This declaration sent a shiver down Brian's spine.

"YOU KILLED OLSON? Seriously?" he stammered in response, in shock now.

"Yes, is there a problem with that?" the smiling killer replied.

"Umm, what do you think?!" Brian blurted out with a combination of force and fear.

"Jeez, Kon. Take it easy. No one will ever figure it out...I made it look like a suicide. Those hicks up there are happy to see the bastard dead. I solved one hell of a problem for you and your future wife, you guys should be thanking me! If I spread the word up there those farm hicks would probably elect me as their mayor!"

The smile on Summer's face was sinister and scary, but Brian settled back and returned the smile despite the fact that his blood now ran cold inside.

"You're unbelievable, you know that?"

"Yes I am." came the killer's response with an air of ego and satisfaction.

Chapter Nineteen

"Take one more look." - Will Alford

Detective Alford pulled into his usual parking spot at seven thirty on a sultry Tuesday morning in September. Minnesota was strange, the summers were hot and humid, but when September arrived one never knew what to expect. The temperature could range anywhere from forty-five to ninety-eight degrees and on occasion one could even expect a stray snow shower at the end of the month.

There would be no snow this fall however and the high temps made Alford, a bigger man, extremely grumpy. He climbed the steps to the government center slowly, feeling his age with every stride. He was seriously considering retirement a better option with each passing day; in fact, the idea was at the forefront of most of his thoughts and plans.

Detective Hoffman had already been at work for the better part of an hour, having downed a cup of coffee and two jelly donuts from the bakery across the street. He was settling into what he hoped would be a slow day. His nights were consumed with Kit, and they were wilder than he had ever experienced.

Sleep was no longer a guarantee, much less an option as they ran wild with their romance. He knew he was in way too deep, there was no going back...Kit was the one. With a smile on his face he pondered whether she felt the same as he did. The young cop was pretty sure the feeling was mutual.

"Hey, rook, what's going on today?" Alford called across to his desk amid a fairly empty room.

"Not much, boss. There has been nothing on the wire and no new files. Everything has come to a crawl." Alford stopped at his secretary's desk and traded gruff greetings with her before he settled in behind his desk in his private office.

He left the door open; it was much more personal this way and he could see and hear what was going on out in the pen. He missed the bullpen, the area where all the detectives worked together and socialized...all the jibs exchanged between the colleagues, a friendly bond that could not be broken. His mind drifted back in time, all his partners were now gone...dead or retired. Being the boss in the office, he was no longer part of the mix and he felt this deep inside. The heartbreak of a lifelong officer.

"Hey rook, commeere..." Alford's phrase blended into a mess of words. Hoffman gave him a strange look, interpreted this slurry sound, and walked to the office door. Alford shuffled through a few papers on his desk, never looking up but well aware of the young detective now standing in his doorway.

"Take a seat for a second." Hoffman methodically dropped into the closest chair and waited for his boss. Alford glanced up and peered over his reading glasses as he began.

"Where are we with the museum case?" Hoffman sat quietly, not wanting to sound lazy or foolish, and then picked his words carefully.

"Sir, there has been very little information to work with concerning the museum. I have stopped in once or twice since our visit and have nothing to report. There is nothing out of the ordinary over there. In fact, I have found Mr. Konrad, the curator, to be very cooperative. He's a good man."

Alford stopped shuffling his paperwork and smiled at the young detective, the realization rushing his mind.

"Your visits wouldn't happen to involve a young lady that works over there, one with a terrific backside, would it?"

Hoffman was caught, he blushed openly and looked away with a sheepish smile.

"Do you think it's a good idea to be loving up to the people we are investigating? For all we know she could be a suspect!"

The veteran detective's words took a serious tone along with the look on his face. The smile vanished from Hoffman as well, he sat quiet and motionless, not knowing how to respond. The younger detective felt like a schoolboy being reprimanded by the principal.

"You had better watch yourself, young man...you could be wandering into a very dangerous situation."

Alford knew the rookie was confused, hurt, and even a bit mad. His face was a mixture of shame and dejection. The older boss softened his tone.

"Just be careful, all right? I'd hate to see anything bad happen to you. We need to wrap this case up as we will be moving on to other things." The young detective relaxed slightly, responding to the paternal words of the older man.

"Do you want me to pursue this case further, or should we wrap it up?" he questioned, hoping for another visit to the museum and Kit. He had no reason to think anything was wrong, but liked hanging out with Konrad and seeing Kit at work.

"Go ahead and stop over, take a look around. Be a detective...behave yourself. If there is nothing we will back off and move on to something else of greater importance. Take one more look."

Hoffman grabbed his badge and sport coat from his desk and headed out into the warmth of the morning sun. *"The case might be over, but Kit and I are just getting started."* he reflected with a youthful smile.

The trip to the museum took less than ten minutes, traffic was unusually light for a Tuesday. Jay found a spot on a side street after completing a couple of laps around the building; Tuesdays were usually very busy days in the museum world. He climbed the front stairs of the building and, after passing the information desk, began to wander with a tour around the main floor.

"Jay! What are you doing here, love?" He turned with surprise as his lover smiled and ran to him. She was beautiful in his eyes and he reveled in his good fortune.

"I just had a little time this morning and thought I would stop on over...I missed you!" Her smile lit up the corridor, people were now staring at the lovers, taking notice of their words and actions.

She moved against him in a loving embrace and they kissed in front of the tour group. A few kids let out 'oohs' as parents tried to turn them away. A lady and gentleman were thought not proper if they showed affection in public, but at this moment this lady and gentleman were caught up in their own world.

After a tender moment, Kit was on her way to finish off delivering paperwork to the third floor and Jay walked over to visit with Brian. Both couples were spending more time with each other and Jay and the young curator had become fast friends. Brian did not have many friends and so this manly relationship, although potentially dangerous, had become special in his life.

Jay peeked into the open door and exclaimed "Hello, friend...how is the world treating you on this fine morning?" Brian looked up with a surprised smile.

"Pretty good, but judging from your meeting with Kit out there it is treating you better!"

Jay stood a little straighter and returned the smile with a bit of bravado. "Things are well."

Deep in the recesses of Brian's mind a thought of concern floated to the surface. *"Why is a detective, although a friend, paying me a visit on a Tuesday morning?"*

Konrad casually scanned his desk looking for anything that could incriminate him. There was nothing to be found. The young curator found himself getting more and more paranoid despite the fact that the business was so slow it was almost nonexistent since his return from New York. *Relax, there is nothing to worry about...he is just a friend.*

"Bri... Brian! Are you in there?" Jay quizzed with a smile as his friend was stuck in a daydream.

"Uh, what was that?" Konrad defensively asked, lost in what was said.

"I was saying, are we still on for the barbeque at the park this weekend? Kit set it up with Annie, it should be a great time. I think they may even be inviting more people from here. Did Annie mention it to you?"

Brian straightened up in his chair a bit and demonstrated confidence and an air of charm.

"Of course, the get-together! It will be grand, we are looking forward to it. She spent half the weekend shopping for it...I hope you will be hungry, she's really doing it up!" Both men smiled and chuckled at their good fortune.

"Well, I had better find the little lady and say goodbye."

Jay excused himself and took a long walk around the museum, checking out the newest exhibits with interest. Although he was no expert at art history, having only taken one course in college a few years ago at the U, he did notice some peculiar things.

Most of the art on the third floor, the newer exhibits, were all from the eastern front. East Germany, Hungary, and the Soviet Union were represented in larger than average numbers within the displays. Dadaism made no sense to Hoffman, but he knew enough about it to equate it with the Communist movement that was sweeping the European and Asian continents.

Why in the world would a museum in Minneapolis, Minnesota be displaying Communist art of all things? There is so much of it...who in the world would even really like this in a Midwestern enclave like this? How in the world does it even get here...so far away from its origin? Why would someone want to display this, with the government taking such a harsh stand against the East? It's so bizarre.

Hoffman knew something wasn't right, he surveyed the empty room, gazing at the origin of the pieces on display. Of thirty-four works of art, twenty-eight originated from an Eastern Bloc country, post World War II. Something was up and he felt a rejuvenated interest to figure it out. *"Money and art, Eastern European and Russian works...interesting!"*

The young detective continued around the museum and before he knew it the lunch hour was upon him. After finding Kit, they walked across the park to a small café and enjoyed a nice, quiet lunch together. Fortunate to find a table outdoors in the shade, both made the most of their hour together.

"Say Kit, I was checking out the art on display up on the third floor...it's really weird stuff. Dadaism...what's the deal with those exhibits?"

Kit chewed thoughtfully on a piece of lettuce and found herself somewhat puzzled as well.

"I don't know, dear. It IS really strange stuff. It comes and it goes, we seem to get a lot of it. It kind of creeps me out a little bit...I don't like to go up there. You know though, Brian really seems to like the stuff. He's always up there and always seems to be ordering more of the stuff."

Jay casually changed the subject to something more positive, but filed this information away in his brain.

Chapter Twenty

"It's Saturday for crying out loud!" - *Jay Hoffman*

Alford sat at his desk in a quiet office on an empty floor of the government center, everyone else having gone home hours before. The information that Hoffman provided him concerning the exhibits at the museum were of great interest. New York's bureau had also sent more files outlining shipments of goods to Minneapolis and points beyond.

More money had been discovered within this trail of goods and one agent was fortunate enough to recover a vile of microfiche in New York. After an examination of the film, the bureau found that plans for a timed detonator on a fusion device were provided in detail, courtesy of a defense plant in the upper Midwest. Detective Alford immediately suspected the Honeywell defense plant in Minneapolis.

The old detective did not say much about this, he kept most of the critical information from Hoffman due to the budding relationship between the young detective and the museum employee. Alford believed that love could cloud good judgement and eventually backfire on the investigation. The young detective was in love, there was no doubt about that. Alford decided to take a late night drive over to the museum and possibly visit the curator at his home.

Grabbing his light overcoat and hat from the stand by his door, he headed across the bullpen and out the door into the chilly air. A light drizzle of rain, hardly perceptive was drifting from the dark sky. The detective carefully watched his steps as he descended to his auto on the street, and after checking his rearview mirror, he sped out into the traffic on his way south.

Wipers squeaking on his windshield, Detective Alford pulled up to the dark curb in front of the museum, its well-lit edifice providing the only illumination. He looked up at the building and worked his way up the long steps. It was well after ten o'clock, chances were that the building was locked up; he checked the large, glass entrance door and found his assumption was correct.

The big man moved back to the sidewalk and took a short walk around the corner to the area where the loading docks were located. There was no movement here either, everything seemed eerily quiet; the museum was all locked up for the night. With nothing happening here, Alford decided to pay the young curator a visit, or at least check out his humble abode.

Brian Konrad lived surprisingly close to his workplace; the detective passed by it before he even realized where he was. Having verified the address from the files with Hoffman, the veteran detective was sure he had found the right locale. Lights were on in the house as Alford parked across the street.

A short wait of ten minutes produced enough movement inside the home to assure him that Konrad was in for the evening. The detective exited his car and took a walk around the block to the alleyway behind Brian's house. He recognized the proper garage belonging to Konrad by viewing the back of his house and he settled in for a moment, not sure what he was looking for.

Alford heard what sounded like whistling far off in the distance. It was a tune that seemed very familiar but he couldn't quite identify it by name. A cat shrieked further down the alley as a garbage can clanged loudly. The muffled noise of a man and a woman having an argument was somewhere near, a house or two away. The light rain had now stopped and a light breeze picked up.

The veteran detective pulled his collar up higher on his neck and stared at the back of the house with a puzzled look. Through the rear kitchen window he could identify at least three people, maybe four sitting at a table and laughing. Konrad was there along with two women, one appeared to be his partner's girlfriend from the museum.

He did not hear the stranger approaching until it was too late. The club crashed down upon his head with a crunch, forcing skull through brain matter. Alford never knew what hit him, he had barely turned before impact and now was quickly dying on the cement behind Konrad's garage. Summers reached into the old man's coat and retrieved the detective's car keys.

Sneaking through Konrad's yard, he made his way out to the street and crossed to Alford's car. The engine turned over and Summers returned to the alley for the body. In less than two minutes the detective went from alive and on a stakeout to dead in the trunk of his car.

Summers removed the wallet from the body, took the cash, and threw it into a backyard on the northside of Minneapolis. The veteran agents' body was found at sunrise by a citizen taking out the trash near Victory Memorial Parkway, miles away from the Konrad residence. William Alford was a victim of an apparent robbery and homicide.

****

Jay Hoffman awoke to the shrill ring of his telephone in the kitchen; he felt like something had died in his mouth. The night before involved consuming too much gin while playing bridge with his friends in their south side home.

He probably should not have driven in his condition, but Kit helped him navigate the streets at two in the morning. She was now passed out next to him and the damn phone would not stop ringing. The shrill noise didn't seem to ever end and he was getting angry.

"Who in the world would be calling me at this time of the morning? Its Saturday for crying out loud!" Kit stirred slightly and turned over; she was in rougher shape than Jay.

He trudged to the kitchen as the phone began again and he picked up with a growl.

"Jay, its Alice." the voice sobbed. "He's gone, he's gone. Someone found him on the north side this morning." The sobbing intensified as the young detective became impatient.

"My god, who is gone?" his voice boomed. The voice on the other end of the phone became a whisper.

"Will is gone. Captain Alford, he's gone. His wife just called me." Jay was silent, speechless, numb. He fumbled the phone slightly as he tried to process what he just heard. "How...how did it happen?" he moaned.

"I don't know...I just got the call myself. They said he was robbed."

The young man was stunned and was having trouble catching his breath. His head, already reeling, was now feeling faint. Jay fought back the urge to vomit on the kitchen linoleum.

"I gotta go, I'm so sorry Alice." He left the secretary on a dead line as he placed the receiver back on the hook.

Hoffman stumbled into a kitchen chair and stared out the window for a moment, he knew he had to go downtown to the office. His head was spinning, his stomach retched and its contents spilled at his feet. The tears poured down his face as he trembled with his elbows on his knees.

The young detective had experienced losing important people before, but he had never lost a partner. His emotions raced as he showered and dressed, eventually hurrying through light traffic to get downtown. He was mad, confused, and filled with sorrow as he entered the bullpen area just after ten o'clock. Most of the detectives were also arriving and no one seemed to have any answers.

As the morning progressed into afternoon the story of the robbery and homicide became much clearer. William Alford was a man in the wrong place at the wrong time. So many questions were left unanswered. The detectives pondered the situation and came to the realization that there was a lot more here than what was apparent.

Detective Jason Hoffman had no idea that his partner was killed less that seventy-five feet from where he was sitting with his friends while drinking and playing bridge the evening before.

Chapter Twenty One

"He thought you were the best of the lot." - Alice

The maintenance men shoveled furiously as if bound by some time constraint while the heavy snow was winning the battle on the steps of the government center. Huffing away, the workers were dressed alike in what looked like military issued gear direct from the arctic tundra. They were making slow progress while remaining courteous to the employees who were hustling up the steps, obviously late for work.

Jay Hoffman was one of the crowd but managed to greet a few of the men by first name; Hoffman valued courtesy and respect. He was grateful that his work took place inside the building and not in the midst of the storm.

The snow had started on Thanksgiving evening and had plagued the Twin Cities for the whole weekend. While he liked the seasons and usually enjoyed the white stuff, this was even too much for him. He silently cursed it as he reached the front doors of the building. Crossing the atrium and taking the elevator to the second floor he began to thaw out.

The drive from his small, modest home in St. Anthony had taken much longer than he expected, the clock was pushing nine and he was usually in by eight or earlier. His lateness also involved Kit, who he left off in front of the museum. She was still on his mind as he crossed the bullpen to his desk.

"Detective Hoffman, can I see you a moment?" Alice called from her former director's office. Jay was still reeling from the death of his superior and partner over a month ago. A temporary administrator from two floors up had taken control of the national crime division, but he was scarcely available. The young detective was pulled from his pleasant thoughts as he entered the warm office.

"Captain Berg called from upstairs...he wants me to deliver a message to you. You are to take over this office today." Alice's voice trailed off a little at the end as her eyes dropped to the floor for a moment. She was still struggling with Captain Alford's death as well.

"What do you mean?" the young detective stammered, surprised by this news.

"This is your office now. Berg promoted you over everyone out there, you have been moved up." she replied softly yet with conviction.

"Me? Why ME?" he continued with confusion. "They'll eat me alive out there...some of those guys have TWICE the experience I do!"

Alice took a step toward him and looked him in the eyes. "Let me worry about those clowns out there. You are the best of the bunch and have earned this, take over and do your best. Will would have wanted this for you, he thought you were the best of the lot."

Hoffman felt a tear form at the corner of his eye but knew that now was the time to remain strong. His tears were shed long ago and he had to move on, as painful as it still was. He had to be strong for Alice too...she believed in him as much as the old captain did. The older woman passed him slowly, never looking away from his eyes as she exited the room and closed the door behind her.

She continued looking at him through the glass and nodded briefly to show belief in her new boss. Jay moved behind the desk and slowly lowered himself into his former partner's chair. He felt as if the old man was still there as he slowly surveyed his new surroundings...it was time to get down to work and he knew where he wanted to start.

Nobody took the time to check in on the new boss and offer congratulations or advice. The men on the floor were gazing at the office and exchanging small talk, most of it bitter, but nobody of authority bothered to stop in and confirm the situation.

Alice reappeared in the early afternoon and dropped an administrative calendar for the week on his desk; there were more meetings than he had expected and this made him a little nervous. The young man had no idea what the new promotion entailed. He started working his way through open case files and found himself bored by three o'clock.

Jay turned toward the window and surveyed the situation outside in an attempt to stay awake. The snow was falling lighter now, maybe the storm would let up. Opening the credenza under the window his eyes suddenly focused on a file that was bulging with papers.

"What could this be?" he muttered with wonderment, thinking that everything he was to work through was in a pile at the corner of his desk.

"Minneapolis Art Institute. Brian Konrad. Interesting."

Picking up the file, he approached the door, opened it and called to his secretary. Alice made her way back into the office and mused "It's getting to be time to wrap things up for the day. What do you have there?"

Jay extended the file toward her. "I was hoping you knew. I found it in the credenza over there." They glanced at the piece of mahogany furniture below the window.

"I have no idea… I have only been assisting on the stuff on the desk. What do you think it is?" she questioned, eyes wider with curiosity.

"It looks like the stuff that Alford and I were working on earlier in the year, the museum case. I thought it was pretty much closed…maybe he just misplaced the file instead of putting it to rest."

"Could be…" the wise secretary replied, "He has been known to do that before." The sadness returned to her face and voice.

"Well, I will give it the once over and take care of it then." The new boss echoed the sadness softly. "That will be enough then. Feel free to take off whenever you feel ready, I'll see you tomorrow."

"Thanks, boss." A proud smile returned to her face.

Returning to his chair, he felt something tugging at the back of his mind…it was if the old man was pushing him to open the file and read its contents. Jay was reluctant, he told Kit he would pick her up at four-thirty from the museum on the south side. Judging from the remnants of the storm it would take him a half hour to get there so he would have to leave soon.

The manila folder sat there on the desk as if it were staring at him, daring him to open it. *"Aww, what the heck, I've got a quick minute."* He peeled back the cover of the folder and was surprised at how many little notes were stuffed in amongst the standard paperwork.

"Hmmm, looks like Alford was still working on this..." It became quickly apparent that the old detective was fixated on Brian Konrad and the museum as well as the Konrad house.

"Konrad under surveillance? Interesting. What did the old man figure out?" Moving through the notes and papers quickly consumed the young detective's interest and before he knew it his watch was pushing four o'clock.

"This can wait until tomorrow." he stated with a finality as he stood up, grabbed his coat and hat, and made for the door. He closed it louder than he expected and jumped slightly, some of the men left in the room gave him a bit of a glare. A few well-wishers gave him a friendly goodbye as he hit the elevator in full stride and from there made his way across the street and out into the messy drive.

She was at the curb waiting patiently in the light snow as he rounded the corner; she was a blonde vision of beauty in his eyes and he smiled at his good fortune. Pulling up carefully, she opened the door, slid across the bench seat, and planted a tender kiss on his lips.

"Hey beautiful! Guess what? I got promoted to bureau captain today!" Surprise filled her eyes and she let out a celebratory squeal as she hugged him.

"Whoa! Take it easy! We're in public you know!" he laughed aloud, beaming with pride.

"I'm so proud of you! I know you'll be perfect!" Kit returned with a glow.

They talked of the day's events as he slowly made his way to drop her off at her apartment, then took another half hour to make his way to the curb in front of his small bungalow. He wished she would move in with him but the neighbors would lose their minds with the idea of a couple living in sin on their block; it was not proper.

Kit dreamed of being at the point where Brian and Annie were and he wished the same thing. He missed her already and wished they would have made plans to go out and celebrate the moment, but the weather and another workday ahead pushed those plans to later in the week.

At the back of his mind, as he trudged through the snow that was piled on his front walk, the thought of Brian Konrad re-entered.

"*Tomorrow will be a busy day.*" he reflected to himself as his key opened the front door to a warm, cozy house.

Chapter Twenty Two

"Maybe things won't be so bad after all."- Brian Konrad

The phone rang on the young curator's desk, snapping him out of a daydream about something fairly insignificant. He was working way too hard lately and was getting much less sleep than he desired. Between work and wedding plans with Annie, he was mentally exhausted. The March wedding was quickly approaching and, despite Annie doing most of the work, he found his mind overwhelmed. Brian picked up the phone on the third ring with fatigue in his voice.

"How's the boy wonder of the art world?" the spunky voice greeted from the other end of the line.

"Evie...how are you?" he replied, his voice livelier. "I will be in town tomorrow for a luncheon and was wondering if you would like to join me? How about it? It will be marvelous!"

The heiress exuded excitement and new life in her attitude. Brian couldn't even consider saying no to her.

"I think that would be wonderful! We can catch up on events of the day!" he confirmed with newfound gusto.

Only after hanging up the phone at the end of five more minutes of excited conversation did he realize that he had just made a date with a woman that he had shared a relationship with. *"Oh shit, what will Annie say about this?!"*

Tomorrow arrived and in a strange way Brian found himself excitedly looking forward to seeing Evie. It was the little things that gave this away, he was checking himself in the mirror and strutting around the museum with a little more swagger than normal. As the time for his luncheon date approached, he headed downtown and found himself fifteen minutes early for their meeting.

The eager curator surveyed the dining room and realized that there wasn't a single person he could place. Total strangers...he started to suspect that this might not be the kind of luncheon he had expected.

Evelyn drifted in through the revolving door at the front of the restaurant and most of the heads in the room turned to check her out. To say she was stunning was the understatement of the year. Brian felt a sense of manly pride flow through him as she approached his table and gave him a long hug and kiss on the cheek. She smiled at him with a sexy confidence and opened the conversation.

"Well, boy wonder, how have you been?" Brian laughed, caught up in her charm. He couldn't help the fact that thoughts of the special night they shared together raced through his mind.

"So, what do I owe the pleasure of your company to this time?" he asked with a sincere tone.

"I miss you, Brian, I really do. I thought it would be wonderful to spend a little time together and catch up on things. I hope you don't mind me calling you...I really miss you."

Evie batted her eyes and pursed her lips, giving off a sexy vibe that Brian enjoyed. *It's nice to be wanted.*

Brian felt himself blushing a little, the young brunette picked up on this immediately; she knew what she was doing to him. *It's working...hmmm.* Her coquettish attitude was radiating.

"I have a special event at the end of this month and I don't have anyone to accompany me. Would you enjoy giving me the honor of your escort?" Evie's smile was absolutely killing him in a wonderful way...he couldn't take his eyes off hers.

"Well, that could be a bit of a problem. You see, I am seeing someone now and we are pretty serious."

He purposely failed to mention the fact that they were engaged. Evie noted this right away and tried to steer clear, not wanting to ruin a great mood at the table. The waitress suddenly appeared and they took a moment to look over the menu. After soliciting advice from her, they placed their order and went back to the business at hand. They continued to glower at each other with affection.

"I'm not about to stand in the way of your relationship. By no means would I intend to do you any harm. I just thought it would be wonderful for us to share each other's company."

Her spoken sexuality was driving Brian crazy. He found his mind wandering into a lustful area along with his eyes; he couldn't help but to check her out. *It's working...he wants ME!* With an excited smile, she continued her pursuit of the man.

"It's really very simple." she cooed. "I need someone to escort me, to be my significant other for an evening, and I think it would be very beneficial for your position at the museum."

He noticed that she openly looked him over with lustful excitement as the drinks arrived.

"If I understand what you are saying, this is a business proposition, right?" he inquired, hoping it might also have a little more significance in her mind.

"If that's what you want to call it, a business proposition it is. Come with me, it will be fun." Her voice was low and sultry again, suggesting a double entendre. Brian Konrad could not resist.

"I think we can make the arrangement to attend together. It will be very good business for both of us." They continued to bask in the glow of each other's presence.

The lunch was superb, there was no doubt that the company enhanced the food, and Brian and Evie parted ways for the day. He returned to a full afternoon of work at the museum as he was expecting a big delivery from Dallas on its way to New York. Summers had tipped him off again that they would be meeting that evening and there would probably be more information making its way to the East.

Brian would be the middle man in the transaction and would transcribe some information for processing further down the line. He would have to designate what goods went on to New York, what would stay in Minneapolis, and what might make its way to Pittsburgh. Pennsylvania was now in the mix again and the steel city was the latest destination to the east.

As Konrad expected, the crate arrived mid-afternoon and Emery called up to announce the parcels' arrival. *"Damn, I'm glad Emery doesn't have a clue about the business. I would have to have to get rid of him...nice kid."* Brian sauntered down to the loading dock and passed Annie on the way.

Guilt suddenly weighed on his mind as he remembered his sinful lunch with another woman. *Annie would understand...it's for the good of the museum.* This attempt to rationalize his lust for Evie had no positive effect on him. He gave Annie a weak smile as he passed her tour group and the guilt still messed him up.

Seeing the large crate at the loading dock entry door shifted his mind to brighter thoughts. *"I wonder what's in this one...it's a big sucker."* Emery approached from his side office and greeted his boss.

"Hello, Mr. Konrad. It arrived a half hour ago...awfully big, isn't it?" Not waiting for his boss' reply, he continued eagerly. "What do you want me to do with it? It's too big to leave out here on the dock."

The crate was over six feet long and three feet wide, it probably weighed in excess of three hundred pounds. "What do you think it is?" the young employee asked with a hint of glee.

"Jeezus, Emery, how in the world would I know? What does it say on the packing slip?" Brian wasn't particularly in the mood for small talk and he knew the packing slip would reveal nothing on this item. Nobody was supposed to know what was inside except for Brian.

"Sir, the slip gives no mention of what's inside other than it's fragile."

"Well then, Emery, let's move it into Bay A. Secure it in the valuables room. Use a forklift, huh, or you'll kill yourself." The boss gave his subordinate a sideways glance and grin.

"Forklift...that's funny boss...you think I'd lift it with my bare hands? Funny, boss." Emery chuckled as he hustled off to secure the machinery to move the huge crate.

Guilt returned as Annie stopped by his office on her way out the door for the day. He kissed her soft lips and she returned the affection with passion of her own. Locked in an embrace for a moment, their eyes locked and Annie asked "What's wrong dear?"

The stressed curator shrugged slightly. "Uh, nothing. I'm just a little worn out today."

She studied him for moment and then gave him a lengthy, warm hug.

"Well honey, don't work too late. I'm heading over to your place to make you a nice dinner, something warm and cozy. Maybe soup?" Brian smiled and nodded. He would be working later than she knew.

Brian watched his fiancée drift across the entryway to the museum and leave through the main entrance. *What in the hell am I doing having lunch with another woman?* The young curator turned to enter his cramped office and knew the answer to that question in an instant. He wanted another evening with Evie.

Five o'clock became Eight o'clock quicker than Brian realized. Summers showed up at the front door and delivered another small vial of microfiche to be shipped on. After a quick greeting and exchange, Konrad hustled inside and opened the vial.

"More technical shit that I don't understand. Must be awfully damned important though...Brooks has been waiting for this for a while now."

Typing the next destination on the packing slip took one minute. Jogging down to the loading dock took another two because no one was left in the museum. Waiting for Loren, the night watchman, to pass took another two minutes and then opening the top of the huge parcel with a crowbar expended another three minutes. The Egyptian sarcophagus inside was a beautiful gold hue, he took another minute to examine and appreciate its beauty.

The museum boss slipped the vial containing important detonator information under the huge item, attached a note to Dr. Brooks, and replaced the lid. The packing slip was firmly attached with packing tape and Brian sprinted back to his office. Annie was going to be mad; he was supposed to be home an hour ago.

Grabbing his coat and hat, he locked his office and made his way out and down the stairs to his automobile on the curb. Brian entered his warm, aromatic home at 8:45 and was greeted by his beautiful bride to be with a kiss and a smile. *Maybe things wouldn't be so bad after all.*

Chapter Twenty Three

"It never hurts to look at a beautiful young woman." -
Mr. Quigley

For all practical purposes, Annie was now moved in with Brian at his house in South Minneapolis. They did their best to hide the fact from the neighbors, but Brian's next-door neighbor, Mr. Quigley, would exchange knowing smiles with the young man when Annie would sometimes appear at odd hours around the house.

Quigley was jealous, he was enjoying looking at the beautiful young woman every chance he could get. *"Lucky young bastard!"* the old auto assembly worker would whisper to himself with admiration of Brian. Quigley had enjoyed these pleasures many years before. Now with Mrs. Quigley passed on and the old man too ancient to enjoy the fruits of youth, he was secretly proud of the successful young curator that was the perfect neighbor. *"It never hurts to look at a beautiful young woman."*

Brian's secret was safe with him. Most of the other neighbors didn't really care much about what was going on. They would sometimes get together during the steamy summer months to socialize, but in the dead of winter they kept to themselves and hibernated from the cold. No one noticed the frisky young couple living together on the quiet parkway on the south side. If no one took notice of the stunning redhead, they certainly wouldn't notice Brian's side involvement with a business that was run from half a world away. Safe times indeed.

A frigid Thanksgiving holiday gave way to the beginning of the Christmas season and Konrad was caught in a dangerous predicament. The event that he was to share with Evie was a dinner party on Summit Avenue in St. Paul. This was a posh neighborhood that oozed of money and historical success.

With an excuse to work late and meet with a donor, he had the alibi he needed for Annie. Evie had phoned him briefly earlier in the week with the address and details; Brian met her downtown at an establishment for a drink and then they headed to their destination.

They arrived amid a flourish of guests; the party was much larger than he had imagined. Neither Evie or Brian seemed to recognize anyone and the event became a bore much earlier than both had expected or wished. Although they didn't seem to mingle with many people, they were enjoying each other's company and before he realized it, Brian began to saunter around in an inebriated state. The cocktails packed a punch and they seemed to hit him much harder than they did Evie. Ten thirty was quickly upon them and Evie suggested they move on with their night. She had plans, big plans.

Brian was questionable as a driver and so Evie volunteered to take the wheel. They maneuvered their way across the Twin Cities and just over an hour later were pulling up in front of the large mansion on Lake Minnetonka. The beautiful brunette didn't have to do much coaxing to get Konrad to follow her into the house and up to her bedroom. Buying a little time to prepare the proper mood, she left Brian alone on her bed as she changed into something more comfortable. The plan was to take his breath away and steal his heart once and for all.

The suave playboy carried up a strong drink that had been prepared downstairs at the bar and was now laying on the huge poster bed with a silly smile on his face. *"I am about to be one very lucky man!"* he mused to himself as he placed the cocktail on the bed side table to his right and unbuttoned the collar of his shirt.

****

The balcony didn't seem that far off the ground, a good leap, a bit of a climb and he could be on it in less than a minute. Up he went, a sense of urgency in his movements; he'd better get there in time or else. Once upon the balcony, the French door opened with ease.

Struggling to catch his breath, he saw Brian lying on the bed, fully clothed but slightly tipsy from a little too much to drink. Summers had noticed a bit of a waggle in his step as Evie led him up the front steps and into the Minnetonka mansion. The young curator had been there before and was anticipating another great evening when everything came to a sudden halt.

"Get yourself up and follow me NOW!" Summers commanded in a whisper that brought fear to Konrad.

"Summers, what the hell?" he whispered back with a bit of alarm.

"Don't ask questions...we have to LEAVE NOW!" The older man grabbed Brian by the upper arm and pulled him up off the bed.

"What do you think you're..."

Summers covered up Konrad's mouth with his hand to quiet the drunken fool. "Take my word...we have to leave NOW!"

His voice raised slightly on the last word and Evie called from the closed bathroom "Is everything OK dear? Is someone there?"

Brian looked into Summer's eyes and sensed that they were in big trouble. The men bolted through the French doors and onto the balcony. Summers led the way, shimmying down the support column and Brian awkwardly followed. Landing off balance and feeling his alcohol, the young man stumbled and then ran for his vehicle in pursuit of his older rescuer.

"Give me the keys." the sober man insisted.

"But I'm OK to drive" Brian countered with a combative smile.

"Like hell you are. Give me the keys NOW!" Summers half shouted. Both men piled into the sedan and left the neighborhood at an unsafe speed. They were onto Minnetonka boulevard before Brian could gather his senses enough to question the crazy series of events.

"Just what was that about? You interrupted a great chance for me to have a little fun." he asked with a slight laugh at the end.

"Fun? How about getting yourself killed? Fun?!" Summers impatience and lack of humor came through.

"Are the Pomeroys aware that you took to breaking and entering on their estate? If they catch you, you are through old Summers. They will hang you high!" Brian laughed as he lectured the older companion.

"Pomeroys? What are you talking about?" Summers stated with alarm mixed with puzzlement.

"I was about to spend a wonderful evening with Evie Pomeroy. You totally wrecked my good time, Summers." Brian was still buzzing, but was now beginning to count the misfortune of this evening.

"Umm, sir, that is not Evie Pomeroy. That's Evelyn KATZ. As in Evelyn Katzenberg." Confusion filled the younger man's mind. The quiet in the car was numbing, the young curator turned to look at the older man driving and his mood turned somber in a hurry.

"You're kidding, right?" he asked, hoping this was all a joke.

"I'm not kidding sir. I thought you knew. I've been guarding you the whole time...I thought you knew." Summers answered in a low tone, noticing the embarrassment in Konrad's voice.

"I'm a fool." An uncomfortable pause of a minute followed as Brian looked out the passenger window, suddenly sobering back to an uncomfortable reality. "Ok, Summers, tell me what the hell is going on."

"Brooks had me follow you, with all the crazy stuff and the Rosenberg situation falling apart he wanted you protected. I saw both of you leave the restaurant downtown and I recognized her from somewhere. I couldn't place her at first, but I figured you knew what you were getting into. If you really knew the situation, you would not have entered that house tonight on the lake. I figured her out pretty quick, we had a dossier on her back East. It didn't take me long to figure out that she was Evelyn Katzenberg, an American operative working for the bureau. She was too close to you and when you went out with her tonight and so I figured something was up... I had to get you out of there." Summers voice lowered in deference to his boss, he didn't want to create any more tension.

After another moment of silence, he continued. "Sir, she set you up, plain and simple. She is probably working with the Pomeroy family... they are patriotic Americans after all. I don't know how she is related to the Pomeroys, or even if she is. I have not figured out why she is part of their clan, so to speak. I just know however, that she is not really Evelyn Pomeroy."

Brian's emotions were surging through his mind. The realization that he had been played meant that the feds were onto him. *Now I'm in real danger... the question is to what extent?*

A further revelation suddenly played into his mind. *I just traded a relationship with a woman who really loves me, who is going to be my wife...for what? Lust?*

"Pull over Summers, NOW!" Summers swerved the car onto the boulevard shoulder and Brian opened the door and leaned out. He emptied his stomach on the pavement amidst tears.

The bodyguard led the young curator into his house after parking the car in the back driveway and secured the premises quickly. With revolver in hand, he returned to a sober but dejected man sitting at the kitchen table.

"Sir, is there anything else you need?"

Brian turned with a sullen look and replied "No, Summers, that will be all. You can go." Summers smiled slightly and nodded.

"With your permission sir, I think I will stake out a spot on your living room couch. We may have some company this evening."

Brian looked at him with a slight edge of fear and surprise. "This is serious, isn't it?" Summers nodded slowly.

"Very well then, make yourself comfortable. I'll bring you a pillow and some blankets. Summers?" The older veteran paused and locked eyes with him.

"Thank you." Brian gently voiced with genuine gratitude.

Chapter Twenty Four

"Soviet or American, men are suckers for a beautiful woman." - Jay Hoffman

It didn't take long for Jay Hoffman to figure out that the jig was up, that Konrad and his crew were on to his game. Evie contacted him very early on a Saturday morning to say that Brian had made a run for it from her house. She saw another man get into the car with him and they sped away; the realization that her cover was blown was pretty obvious.

The young detective was going to have to find a way to protect the Pomeroy family as well as the beautiful American spy. The Soviet network must have already been aware of the situation with Konrad even though it was pretty certain that the young operative did not suspect a thing until his rescuer came along.

Evelyn Katzenburg was a plant, plain and simple. The Minneapolis bureau was working hard to combat the Reds and one thing led to another. The Pomeroy family was more than happy to comply with requests from Washington D.C., they traveled in the highest social and political circles in America. It paid to know people in high places and when those people asked for favors, you were certain to oblige them. The wealthy family knew little of the actual plan but went out of their way to accommodate the beautiful agent for a price.

The Federal Bureau of Investigation in Washington D.C. had been monitoring the Midwest situation and had figured out a way to plant their agent. Young, beautiful, and extremely intelligent in the aspects of detective work, Evelyn Katzenburg was the perfect agent to handle the Twin Cities. With ammunitions plants and technology companies in this region, Minnesota was home to developments and information that would be vital to the Soviet regime and their race for atomic power.

Geographic location also played a part in placing Miss Evelyn here; it seemed to be that there was a good amount of intel possibly passing through the region. It was enough to convince the Pomeroys that their international food business might be in danger as they would then be eager to take in the determined agent and provide her with the cover necessary to pursue a more dangerous scheme. The prominent family would never know the real reason why she was in Minnesota or who she would be pursuing.

Who is the rescuer and how did he know so much about Evie? Questions started to work their way through

Hoffman's mind as he sat as his desk in the quiet, cold office. There was no way Konrad was going to figure things out, they had covered their tracks. Alford probably never knew about the plan, but the new captain had been working with Washington D.C. for the better part of the month and had come to realize that the Feds had developed a spy program that was a secret to everyone in Minneapolis as well as New York, Dallas, and Philadelphia. The system was run in such a covert manner that there was no way anyone in the Eastern bloc could figure it out.

Hoffman did not have the security clearance necessary to realize that the spies in New York City were only a few blocks away from their enemy's headquarters. The communist fortress was so secure that few if any federal agents knew of their existence. Soviet agents had files on most of the American spies abroad and at home in the U.S; once Summers saw and recognized Evie the game was over. A quick call to New York confirmed her identity in the nick of time. Brian was temporarily spared from being outed himself. One problem still existed...Evie still wanted the young curator.

The Minnesota Museum of Art spy case had taken over every moment of Jay Hoffman's life.

Does Brian know that I'm deep into the case? That I was working with Evie over the last month to set him up? Kit and Annie are still friends...is Brian still trusting of me?

The young detective was no fool. The game that they were playing could get one or both of them killed.

Carefully sifting through the case file for the hundredth time, he pondered his next move. Hoffman was pretty sure that Konrad could no longer be outed by a love interest, he would be too cautious now. It was a plain shame to the detective, for he knew that the love interest angle almost always worked.

"Soviet or American, men are suckers for a beautiful woman."

Evie Katz was given a direct order from her superiors in D.C. to break off all contact with Konrad and go into protective hiding. She was supposed to report to D.C. immediately and the F.B.I. would ensure that the Pomeroy family would be protected. The enormous lake home in Minnetonka would be under constant protection as well, the feds could take no chances of anything dangerous or deadly happening in a suburban area as elite as Tonka.

The U.S. feds had one big problem. Evie was not about to give up on Brian Konrad, much less this case. This was supposed to be her big break. She was determined to get her man one way or another, either at the altar or in jail. The beautiful Ms. Katzenburg had fallen head over heels in love with Brian Konrad.

The young museum curator was frightened to his core. Things were never supposed to get this crazy, this dangerous. Dr. Brooks had all but assured him that there was very little risk in this operation, his chances of getting caught were next to nothing.

The situation began to change when Julius and Ethel Rosenberg, along with family members, were run up on espionage charges. As the case unfolded and Julius was implicated as the leader of an extremely dangerous spy ring, the feds widened their circle of inquiry and began to uncover much more than they had ever dreamed of. Brian Konrad was a cog in a much bigger machine than the one that Julius Rosenberg was running.

How bad can this get? Rosenberg might get the chair. What will happen to me and Annie? Is she in danger? How much do the Feds know? What about Jay...he works for the police...does he know anything? Is Summers right about Evie? Where is Evie? Is it time to run for it? Where would I run too? How come Brooks hasn't contacted me...does he know about this?

The questions flooded Brian's mind, putting him in an almost paralyzed state. Sleep was rare now; he was fighting to think clearly. Annie was noticing a difference in his demeanor and her questions posed to him signaled a concern that was starting to take a toll on their relationship. The young beauty sensed that he was hiding a lot of important stuff.

Everything boiled over in their world on a frigid, icy Saturday morning a week before Christmas.

Sitting quietly at the breakfast table, Annie stared at the shell of a man she was madly in love with a month before. Now she wasn't sure how she felt, but she knew it was different than before.

"What are you hiding?" she asked quietly across the table. Silence engulfed the room. Feeling cornered and with panic rushing through his mind, Brian played it cool and gave no answer. He just stared back at her with a deadpanned gaze. "You're not the same man lately. You're *different*. Tell me what's going on."

Brian was trained to be strong, but this was too much. The woman that he loved, the one he was about to give up a month earlier, the one he was beyond fortunate to have was now putting everything on the line. He could tell this by the tone of her voice, her expression, her stare.

The young man crumbled and in a matter of moments revealed his position in what could be the most dangerous espionage case in American history. "I am part of a Soviet spy ring." He tried to skim over some of the serious parts, but she just sat across the table in absolute shock, a look of disbelief painted on her face.

Annie said nothing. The silence was deafening. Brian said nothing. their eyes met and Annie teared up. She heard nothing that Brian was saying in an effort to console her. She slowly rose from her chair and left the kitchen. The disillusioned woman climbed the stairs in a state of shock and locked the bedroom door behind her. Dropping onto the bed as lifeless as a corpse, she let everything out and cried like she had never cried before. An hour passed and Brian sat motionless at the breakfast table. He wished he had never started this venture, he wished he were dead.

Nearing late afternoon, Annie descended from the upstairs and found her fiancé sitting quietly on the couch in the living room.

"I will stand by you. I will protect you. I love you, I have loved you since I first met you, and I will love you forever." She stood in front of him, declaring her loyalty to him. Brian broke down as she sat down next to him and took him in her arms.

"We need a plan. We need to get you out of this mess. We need to get US out of this mess." With that declaration, the mood turned as they hatched the plan that would hopefully save them both.

****

A young detective sat on his couch with the love of his life cuddled against him as the radio softly played in the background. Something very holiday-like by Bing Crosby; Kit lightly hummed along. Jay Hoffman's mind drifted and then focused on the case that wouldn't leave him alone. Kit stopped humming and looked up at him with a puzzled expression. He repeated softly over and over "I need a plan. I need a plan."

Chapter Twenty Five

"Do it now or it will be too late." - Summers

Summers was discontent with life. The situation he was in changed from one of leadership to one of babysitting the young curator. The thought of Brian Konrad began to bother the older man, he was reminded of the things that the young man had that he did not.

Jealousy began to play in his head along with regret. There were so many times where he could have 'had it all' and yet for some reason his dreams never came true. Summers was beginning to face the fact that he was too much of a drifter; a man with a work ethic that wouldn't allow success.

Money wasn't a problem, happiness was. Spending a better part of his fifty years striving for all the good stuff that life had to offer had left him empty handed. Sure, money could provide pleasures that would temporarily fill one's desires, but there was no long-term plan or future for him. It was time to do something drastic, *to be somebody*, and all it would take would be one simple phone call. *"Do it now or it will be too late."*

A smile crept over his face as he suddenly felt a mysterious relief. He knew who Jay Hoffman was because he had been following Brian around. Hoffman had been staking out the young curator over the past few weeks and Summers prided himself on the fact that nothing ever escaped his attention. He had Hoffman figured out within about an hour of the first stakeout. Summers was supposed to protect Brian Konrad and he performed his duty very well.

With the Rosenberg situation falling apart and Evie being discovered, Summers knew the business would go into a long holding pattern as Dr. Brooks would try to hide the program and figure out how to keep the money stream alive. The cash payouts would no longer involve Summers, at least not in the way it had before. Things were about to slow down and get very tight financially and this frightened the old spy.

The phone rang on Jay Hoffman's desk on the Wednesday after Christmas and the weary young detective answered it with hesitation. *"Who in the world could this be...do I really want to answer this?"*

The young captain was ten minutes away from hitting the front door, twenty away from picking up Kit, and a half hour away from the warm comfort of his home in St. Anthony Village. He picked up the receiver on the fifth ring with disgust in his tone.

"Hoffman." There was a small, distinct pause on the other end before Summers began.

"Yeah, are you the cop working on the museum case? The one with the Konrad guy?" Hoffman sat straight up in his chair and pulled closer to his desk while fumbling to grasp the case file for MMA.

"Yeah, that's me. What can I do for you?" he responded with a controlled tone, not wanting to seem too eager.

"I have information you are going to want...you will need this. There's a catch though." Hoffman rolled his eyes; hoax calls were a dime a dozen.

"There always is...what's the catch?" Momentary silence took over the phone line again.

"I am willing to give you what you need in exchange for no prosecution on me. I've been involved... I want out. Information, assistance, whatever it takes...but I have to have my freedom. Guaranteed immunity."

"I can't guarantee a thing...I'm a captain in the detective unit. Even If you are legit, I can't make a promise like that."

Silence again. It was Summers' turn with this intricate dance. "Ok, whatever. You had your chance." Hoffman panicked as he lost contact with the caller.

A lead this enticing could be too good to pass up. He slammed the phone down with a curse word and Alice looked up from her typewriter with a scowl...she didn't tolerate offensive language. The young captain called her into his office.

"Alice, how would a person go about getting immunity for an informant who may have committed a serious crime?" She chuckled slightly as she looked her boss over.

"What did you do now?" He returned her laugh and continued.

"Say a person is a criminal and has information, very important information that could break a major case wide open. How do I cut a deal to get the facts while keeping him out of jail?"

Alice became more serious, she used to enjoy giving advice to Alford before he passed on. Now the kid was relying on her and it felt good to be needed.

"Tell you what I'd do. I would call upstairs to Bruce Richardson. Bruce is the legal counsel for our department. He's sharp as a tack and will know the answer. I guarantee he will help you. You'll like him too. He reminds me of a more refined version of Captain Alford."

Her voice lowered and her expression went somber at the mention of their former partner and friend. "Do you think he's in now?" the young detective asked with newfound hope. "Call upstairs, give him a try." she recommended with gentleness in her tone.

Hoffman dialed the switchboard and was connected quickly. After a brief conversation with the prominent attorney, the detective realized that there were plenty of ways to get the situation on track...all of them legal. The largest question remained as he hung up the phone. *Is he going to call back?*

Jay knew what he would have to do, what he could offer the man in exchange for his information, and this made him smile as he left the office for the day. With a bounce in his step, he had the lead he needed to crack the biggest case of his life.

Summers called again the next afternoon and Hoffman picked up right away. "Hoffman, did you figure out how to protect me?" Summers snarled over the phone with a hint of sarcasm.

The young detective kept his composure as he now had a number of possibilities. "You need help as much as I do...if you didn't you wouldn't be calling to make a deal." The old spy grumbled a response that Jay couldn't make out.

"Listen, here's how we are going to do it. I'm going to give you a number to a lawyer. If you don't trust me, get your own, but this guy is good. His name is Paul Marquardt, he's a defense lawyer over in St. Paul. He has worked with my guy on a number of deals like this before…he's good and he won't screw you. Contact him with your situation and then he'll contact us and set everything up."

It was deathly silent on the other end of the line. Hoffman wanted to shake the caller up a little bit and wanted to show no nervousness or urgency and so he gave the phone number and promptly hung up without waiting for a response. It was cold, but very effective.

Summers was surprised at the abruptness of the call. He barely had time to say or process anything before it was over. He did have the attorney's number though and with the understanding of client/attorney confidentiality, he knew he could at least make contact with the guy.

"If Rosenberg's brother-in- law could steal secrets from Los Alamos and get off free by turning on his family, this will be easy." He called the number he was given and set up an appointment for the following Monday morning.

"If Brooks finds out, I am dead. What a way to start the new year. Flipping sides…who would have thought it."

Chapter Twenty Six

"Maybe he doesn't know about me." - Evie Katz

Brian and Annie brought in the New Year with style at a party hosted by the museum. Jay Hoffman attended with Kit and everyone had a wonderful time. The young detective caught himself exchanging glances with the young curator and both wondered what the new year would bring in regard to their friendship and fate.

It was easy to surmise that Jay felt much more confident than Brian. Kit and Annie spent most of the evening socializing with colleagues and talking about the upcoming wedding ceremony that was being planned at the museum. It was agreed by all that Brian and Annie's wedding would be the social event of the year.

The second week of January brought in a cold front that one could only find in Minnesota or Siberia. The temperature dropped to twenty below and the winds seemed to constantly howl. Every time a person left the comfort of their dwelling they were taking their lives in their hands; one could freeze to death in a matter of minutes if not properly clothed.

Both couples found themselves hunkered down in their homes when not at work. The Rosenberg trial captured most of the headlines along with congressional committees that were investigating all sorts of people with supposed Communist ties. Hollywood's biggest celebrities were now starting to be dragged into what could become a witch hunt.

There was no business between New York, Minneapolis, and all points west. Everything was halted after the discovery of Evie Katz. The pipeline of information would have to start up again, but caution was the wise choice. Dr. Brooks and his associates would take their time. The Soviet nuclear program was advancing at great speed and all of their bomb tests were going very well. If saving the program meant taking a little time off, that was what they were going to do.

Summers 1869 made his trek to St. Paul, met with Paul Marquardt, and was promised his freedom in exchange for all the information that he could provide on the Soviet spy game. Summers trust was built up and he spilled the beans on most of the operation. At that point, the attorney thought it necessary to bring Hoffman and Brian Richardson into the affair and so a meeting at the downtown police station was arranged.

With all four men at the table, a deal was struck and it was agreed that Summers would flip and become an informant for the feds. Legal documentation was signed and conditional immunity was granted. With this deal in place, the attorneys were no longer needed and Jay Hoffman began to build his plan to break the spy ring wide open.

Summers would continue to be the bodyguard for Brian Konrad. After a thorough rundown of the part of the operation that Summers was aware of, they decided to gather enough evidence to prosecute the young curator as well as the wise, old ringleader in New York. Everything was to be written down with times and dates. All pertinent information had to be kept for future use in court.

Hoffman, with Federal assistance, would direct Summers and keep contact with him away from the museum. In the museum, Summers would be on his own. The Evie situation demonstrated a loyalty between Konrad and Summers and so it was noted that there was little if any danger to the new informant. Both men parted and went to work with the new plan.

The phone rang in Brian Konrad's office. He was overwhelmed with work on a new exhibit and answered in a stupor. "Brian Konrad here."

"Brian. It's Evie. How are you?" Brian felt as if he had been hit on the side of his head by a ten-pound maul.

"Uh, Evie. I'm...ok. How are you?" He didn't know what to say.

"You left me so quickly...things were just getting good. What happened? Why did you run off?" She was fishing for information, wondering how much Konrad knew about her. Brian played it cool.

"I didn't feel well. I had too much to drink and my conscience got the better of me. I couldn't stay...I would be cheating on Annie. We're getting married, you know?" He hoped his acting was adequate.

Maybe he doesn't know about me? Evie pondered to herself as she listened to him. Hope filled her mind for a moment. "I understand dear. You do know how I feel about you, right?" she offered with tenderness.

"Listen, Evie. I don't know if we can ever have this happen again..."

"Oh, I know dear...I just want you to be happy. You know I can make you happy, right? I can give you so much...the family fortune and beyond."

Brian sat back in his chair realizing that she was still moving on him. *She must not suspect a thing!* The young temptress was pushing him around and was feeling confident. Maybe she wouldn't have to leave, maybe she could have him yet?

Brian was confused and couldn't figure the situation out. He tried his best to get rid of her in a hurry so that he could analyze what was happening.

"Listen Evie, I have to go, I have an important guest waiting outside my door. I can't keep him waiting any longer. We'll talk again soon, ok?"

With those last words he hung up the phone and shivered with fear. *"What in the world does she want? What is she up to?"*

He had to get some fresh air, he felt like he was suddenly suffocating. As he exited his office for the front entryway, he passed Annie and must have looked a mess.

"Honey, are you alright? What's wrong?" Concern fell over her lovely face. She moved to him to give comfort and he sidestepped her and ducked out the door.

Annie followed him onto the marble landing and hugged his right arm as she gauged his expression.

"I'm ok, dear. Just feeling a little claustrophobic in my tiny office." She felt sympathy and agreed with her man.

"Someone of your stature deserves a much better workspace. You should move back up to the third floor and take one of the bigger offices...your old one is still open, you know?"

Brian pulled his fiancée close and gave her a warm hug; the temperature outside was freezing and neither had a coat. "I'll be ok. It's nothing major. Just needed some fresh air...and you."

He leaned in and kissed her, she made no attempt to resist his move and kissed him back. They exchanged smiles and re-entered the warmth of the building.

The office was the last place he wanted to be, he had to move around and get his mind working. The couple made a long lap around the second level of the museum, looking over each of the exhibits with a casual gaze, and Brian started to worry even more.

It's one of two things. She's reeling me in for the kill. Either she will try and get me in a situation where I give her information to use against the organization, or she will try to move between Annie and me to win me over. Either her job or her heart, huh? Brian snapped out of his inner mind to see Annie staring at him with a puzzled look.

"You are really lost today. Is something wrong?" Brian moved a step closer and, with a quick look around the room to make sure it was empty, sat both of them on a bench against an art covered wall.

He cautiously whispered "Evie Pomeroy is an American spy. She's not even a Pomeroy. She's tracking me...Summer's figured it out." Annie's eyes lit up with the realization of sudden danger.

"Oh my god, are you sure Summers is right? How does he know?"

Both Annie and Brian cast a quick gaze around the room to make sure they were alone.

"Summers has been tailing me...Brooks ordered him to, and he saw her at one of the events. He recognized her right away. Her real name is Evelyn Katz...short for Katzenburg. She's in the information system in New York...Brooks knows her too."

Confusion and fear rained down on Annie's mind; she started to hyperventilate and fought to regain her composure. Brian gently rubbed her back in hopes of helping her calm down.

"So... is it time to put our plan into action? Time to move?" she questioned uneasily. The young curator paused, not wanting to alarm his fiancée.

"It may be. I have to talk to Summers as soon as possible. Evie called me on the phone this afternoon and I can't figure out what she is up to."

The couple fell silent in the marble corridor, worried that someone might overhear them and turn them in. Brian pretty much had the American spy figured out but he wasn't about to tell Annie what he thought. She would go crazy and would probably hunt Evie down with deadly intention.

"Let's get out of here before someone hears us." Brian helped Annie off the bench and they retreated to his office. Shutting the door, they began to run through their plan.

"I'm going to have to reach Summers as soon as possible. He will need to know what is happening and he will contact Brooks. You go ahead and start things on your end, I will get things going on mine. I'll meet you at home around five, we can talk more then." Annie rose up and left in a bit of a concerned daze. In her mind, the situation was now deadly.

Konrad had to take the chance, he had to call Summers. Waiting for the signal and the next meeting might be too late. *If Evie knows all about me, who else knows? We could all be in danger. We could all get the chair.*

The phone picked up on the second ring, Summers sounded cheery.

"Summers, Brian here. We need to meet." Konrad realized that using their names was dangerous enough, but proposing a meeting could be their demise.

"What seems to be the problem, young man?" the older spy replied with gusto. Brian's mind suddenly reeled a bit. *What In the world, is he drunk?* Brian didn't know whether to respond or not as Summers was acting very peculiar. He decided to risk it.

"The usual place, as soon as you can get here." The older spy was quick to agree on the meeting, it could prove fruitful.

"Right then, I will be on my way. See you shortly."

Summers chuckled after he put the receiver back on the hook. *"He must be worrying about Evie. She must still be in contact with him. What else could it be?"* he mused aloud, enjoying his newfound amnesty. "A visit I will make!"

Summers drove over to the museum and was sitting across from the young curator less than an hour later. It was time to gather some information on the spy to set him up.

Chapter Twenty Seven

"Just follow the plan...just follow the plan."- Brian Konrad

Brian and Annie had settled on a wedding date, the third weekend of March. The museum would be the host and the guest list was growing out of control. On the first Monday of the month the plan began to move.

A letter jump-started the process. Brian had been summoned to Washington D.C. to appear in front of the Committee on Un-American Activities. This letter came out of the blue and scared the hell out of him. Someone somewhere had given his name out to the authorities and something must have happened because now he was about to enter the spotlight, a spotlight he had dreaded.

Summers arrived at the museum well after the close. These meetings had become routine over the last year and a half. Loren, the night watchman, let him into the main lobby without a clue of what was going on. Brian turned the corner to the entry of the museum and greeted Summers casually.

"Good evening Summers, it's good to see you."

Summers smiled coolly but had butterflies inside. "Hello, Mr. Konrad. How are you?" Brian looked at Loren briefly with a smile and turned his attention back to his guest.

"Please join me in my office. Thank you, Loren, carry on."

"Yes sir, have a good evening." the night watchman responded with professionalism.

Summers followed Brian into the small office and closed the door behind him. Both men settled into chairs across the small desk from each other. Brian produced a letter from his breast pocket and slid it across the desk.

"Ah, you have one also. I was wondering if I was the only one. What do you make of this? Are we in danger?" Summers posed these questions with a worried expression on his face.

Konrad was a little surprised that his ally had also gotten a summons. "So, they want us both? Interesting. Brooks hasn't said anything...have you heard from him?" Brian questioned back hesitantly. Summers was playing it cool as he had not gotten a letter but had expected the one for Konrad.

"I haven't heard a thing. I only got mine yesterday. When did you get yours?" Brian looked Summers in the eyes, judging his trustworthiness. "My letter came late last week. I haven't been able to reach Brooks... he hasn't returned my calls. I intend to go to Washington as the letter directs. I assume you will do the same?"

The worry never left Summer's face. He studied the top of the worn desk as he pondered his answer. His acting job was very convincing as he offered "I will probably go to Washington; I mean if we don't, we'll probably look guilty and end up in jail. I really want to wait and see what Brooks has to say. He will know how to handle this better than both of us. But yes, I will probably head to Washington with you."

The men looked over the letter in silence as it lay unfolded on the desk. The official looking document gave the directive to travel directly to Washington D.C. on the third Monday in March. That was cutting it close, Brian and Annie were to be married the following weekend. This could mess a good thing up. The men finally parted, both determined to fix the situation in D.C.

****

Over the next two weeks Brian did his best to keep a normal routine at the museum. Wedding plans continued despite the possible problem, and Annie made sure to keep things moving among her colleagues as well. The soon to be newlyweds led a completely different life away from the museum.

Plans were rehearsed, all alternatives to any conceived situation were reviewed. Annie and Brian worked frantically with the realization that their future life together depended on the plan working to perfection. One wrong move could land them in prison and eventually in the electric chair.

The third Monday in March arrived cold but clear. The air was tense, there was a nervousness present as Brian and Annie loaded the trunk of his sedan with a couple of suitcases of their best clothes. A few important belongings filled another suitcase and eighty thousand U.S. dollars was secured in a sturdy briefcase.

At three o'clock in the morning nobody would suspect what was going on, it was cold and quiet when the last of their stuff was carried quickly out of the house to the garage and loaded. As scared as the couple was, there was also an air of excitement that could not be denied. Brian and Annie snuck back into the house and spent what could be their last few hours together.

The young curator had made it known to his employees that he was taking off for the East coast on the third Monday in March. He let them know that he would return by Friday, the day before the Wedding, for rehearsal. The museum made the necessary adjustments for his absence, this wasn't the first time he would be gone on business. The curator traveled frequently and so everything seemed standard to all of the people in charge of the operation of the museum.

Brian packed a small suitcase and put on his Sunday best as he prepared to make his way to the Milwaukee Road Depot downtown. Annie bid him a teary goodbye as he left his house, planning to stop quickly at the museum before departing herself.

Jay Hoffman knew that the letter had arrived, he'd marked this day on his mental calendar. All he had to do was make sure that Konrad went to Washington and nowhere else. Maintaining a safe distance, the young detective followed Brian over to the museum and parked a half block away. Watching the curator from across the park, he had no reason for alarm. *Probably just picking up a few things and saying goodbye to a few people before the trip.*

Brian indeed said goodbye to a few of his closest employees, they had no idea this was to be a final goodbye, and he made his way to his car in a hurry. Missing the train would mess up the plan. As he descended the grand stairs at the front of the building his eyes caught sight of Annie.

Their eyes locked for a brief moment and he nodded confidently to her. She had everything she could do not to break down; she knew she had to remain strong. Brian climbed into his sedan and sped off to downtown Minneapolis to catch a train.

Konrad arrived at the tan brick structure at 8:47, he had over a half hour before the Washington bound train would leave. Trying to hide his nervousness, he checked the schedule quickly and noted that Great Northern 135 was on time and would be boarding shortly.

Brian surveyed his surroundings and purchased a small cup of coffee at the lounge counter. His pocket a nickel lighter, he looked for anyone he knew, Evie included. He saw no one, but felt the presence of someone following him. *"Just follow the plan...just follow the plan."* he silently repeated to himself over and over with a nervous smile.

Detective Hoffman knew the train schedule, he had checked it the day before and confirmed it by phone earlier that morning. He knew about the letter because he had initiated the proceedings after working with Summers for a month. The detective also knew that Brian Konrad would probably not be coming back from D.C., this was the beginning of the end for the young curator.

Jay knew he was doing the right thing, but deep down he also was saddened by the prospect of losing a friend. The men had become close due to their girlfriends being best friends and with the wedding approaching they were best buddies. *Annie will be heartbroken, Kit also, when he doesn't come home.*

With the call to board, Konrad rose up the steps of the passenger car and presented his ticket as the conductor passed by. Everything was in order. He settled in his seat, placed his suitcase at his feet, and looked out the window.

Far off in the distance, further back in the concourse, Brian thought for a split second that he saw Jay Hoffman looking at him. As quick as he seemed to appear, he was gone. The tense traveler knew it wasn't his imagination, his good friend was checking on him. Jay Hoffman was the enemy now.

What are the odds that he gets on this train and tails me all the way to Washington?

Brian kept a strict lookout. The detective would have a hard time boarding the train without being noticed...the area was too wide open. As the whistle blew and the train began to move, Brian thought he saw Jay looking at him with a smile. There was no mistaking it this time, Hoffman was making sure that Washington was the destination.

Hoffman has no idea about the plan, if he did he'd be sitting next to me right now with a set of handcuffs connecting us. Brian chuckled for a moment at the thought and then became serious again. *Just stick to the plan.*

"Hello friend. Are you ready to ride to D.C.?"

Brian turned suddenly, startled by the voice. Summers settled in next to him after stowing a small travel bag above.

"Hello Summers, how are you this fine day?" Brian greeted, staying very calm. After a minute of small talk to pacify the passengers around them, Summers changed the subject.

"If I calculated everything right, we should be back by the end of the week, possibly Thursday. ABE doesn't seem worried at all. I spoke with him last night. All of this seems to be nothing more than a formality, a wrap up to the Rosenberg situation. ABE thinks we will all be in the clear."

Summers whispered the last comment with confidence. Brian settled back, comfortable with this information.

All of this is probably nothing, Brian thought to himself, but *there is no room for Summers in the plan. I'll lose him in St. Paul.*

Brian had considered that this might take place, that someone might be tailing him. Summers wasn't a tail in his mind, but Brian knew that there was no way to involve the older spy this late in the game. *Summers will be fine, ABE said so himself. No harm.*

Great Northern 135 pushed its way to the Union Depot in St. Paul to pick up more passengers headed east. Both cities bordered each other and so the passengers had barely gotten settled before they arrived at the larger depot. Konrad waited for the train to come to a complete stop, left his suitcase at his seat, and whispered to Summers.

"I just spotted an old college friend back there." He made a wide gesture with his right arm. "Excuse me a moment, I'll be right back. Just want to say hi."

Summers turned his head toward the back of the car and, seeing nothing suspicious, turned his gaze back to the front. "Very well."

Konrad strode nonchalantly through the passenger car to the mail car behind. The luggage he was leaving was insignificant, it was a prop in case trouble arose. If Hoffman or anyone else was following him, now was the time to lose them. He knew that mail would be coming aboard along with carriers to sort it as they moved to the coast.

Opening the door slightly, he looked to his right and found the loading door wide open. He quickly slipped out the door and down the wooden ramp. A quick turn to his left and he was now moving toward the rear of the train and toward a lobby area.

He looked both ways quickly and, with no sign of trouble, he sauntered confidently toward the main terminal. A destination, any destination that would take him west would do. He knew which ride to catch, Annie had scouted it for him. She even purchased the ticket under an assumed name...Mitch Miller.

Brian chuckled as he boarded another Great Northern for the west coast. Summers began to panic when the final call to board was issued at St. Paul.

"Where the hell is Konrad?" he whispered to himself, suddenly fearful. *"His suitcase is right here...he should be back by now."*

The giant locomotive began to groan and move from the station. The older spy looked behind him and then to the front again. The young spy was nowhere to be found. Brian's train was pulling out of the station in the opposite direction. Brian kept a silly smile on his face as he headed back to Minneapolis and beyond.

"Too bad Washington, too bad suckers, I'm out of here!"

Chapter Twenty Eight

"You'll be frying in the chair!" - Jay Hoffman

Brian knew he didn't have a lot of time to wait for Annie. He also knew deep down that he had covered his tracks well. In his mind, it would be almost impossible for Hoffman to track him. Summers would be in a panic and would probably contact Brooks at the next possible stop, somewhere near the Minnesota/Wisconsin border.

The engine pulled into the same Minneapolis depot that Konrad had left less than an hour ago and he saw Annie waiting in the parking lot with his sedan. The plan was working and he felt his heart pounding with joy and excitement.

Jay Hoffman's phone rang on his desk a little after ten in the morning and he picked up right away. "Jay...Summers here. I've lost him. He ditched me in St. Paul at the depot. He just walked off."

Hoffman felt a surge of rage and panic as he listened to the double agent. "If you're double-crossing me, I will have your hide. You'll be frying in the chair!"

Summers became suddenly apologetic and scared of his new boss. "No, no. I wouldn't do that. He got up and left, said he was going to talk to someone he recognized. He even left his suitcase next to me. He just disappeared."

The young detective rocked forward and placed an elbow on his desk, messaging his left temple while holding the receiver in his right. He felt a migraine coming on.

"So where do you think he is?" the detective demanded of his failed agent.

"He either took a line north from here or west back to Minneapolis. I didn't see anything leaving near us when we took off. He might have run off, met up with someone, or just got chicken."

Summers fell quiet, not quite knowing what to believe. "Where are you now?" Hoffman asked.

"Hastings."

"Are you sure he's not on the train with you yet?"

"No boss, I checked everywhere on the way over here. Even asked the car porter."

The officer was working hard to hold it together and not lose his temper. "Get back here and check in with me as soon as you can. I'm going to get things started...just hurry back."

Hoffman slammed the phone down and rose from his chair. In a nervous flurry, he tried to figure the puzzle out as he paced wildly back and forth a half dozen times.

Stopping to jot some notes on a couple of pieces of paper, he then left his office for the bullpen and grabbed two officers. "You... take this and go to this address and look for anyone who would be living there. Tell me if you see a dark sedan with this plate number at the house. Call me after you arrive, call it in through dispatch if you have to." The officer grabbed his standard issue coat and hat and hurried out the door.

Hoffman felt like a fool who was being played as he pivoted toward the second cop. "I'm sending you over to the MMA to check on the hostess. She's medium height, slim, very attractive with red hair, her name is Annie Rogers. Let me know if she is there. Get there as soon as you can, its urgent!" The officer grabbed his gear and headed out as well.

The worried detective started running through all the possible scenarios in his mind and settled on a plan quickly. He knew time was critical and he knew where to start. Moving with haste, he took off for the Minneapolis Milwaukee Road Depot three blocks away.

Brian disembarked from the train with calm confidence and checked his surroundings as only a well-trained spy could do. He casually made his way out to the parking lot and found Annie waiting in his car. He opened the driver's door, slid across the bench seat, and pressed a passionate kiss on Annie's lips.

After a moment of enjoying each other, he started the auto and slowly pulled into the traffic heading south on Washington Avenue. The lovers were now together on their journey to escape the United States and law enforcement.

Hoffman arrived at the depot on foot, knowing exactly what he had to find. He walked the expansive parking lot and curb along Washington Avenue looking for the dark sedan.

If his car is here, we will check the departure board in the depot. No car, no train travel. I hope the car is still here.

The detective had no success in finding the car and silently cursed his poor luck. This endeavor had just become more difficult. Hoffman combed the expansive parking area another time to no avail. A curse word pierced the cold air, directed at no one in particular.

Although he might not be traveling as fast, he could go almost anywhere with the car. If he was traveling by rail, he could be easily traced and intercepted.

Jay's worst fears were pretty much confirmed; if Brian Konrad was running he would be very hard to find.

He entered the depot and went directly to the manager's office. After displaying his badge and explaining his situation, he used the office phone to call the museum. He asked for his girlfriend and was connected a moment later. "Kit, it's Jay. Have you been there all morning?"

"Hey baby, how are you?" she purred, happy that he called.

"Listen, this is important! Is Annie there?"

Kit became annoyed over the fact that the call didn't focus on her. "Why?!" she snapped back.

"Look. I have to know if she is in the museum this morning...it's important." Kit took a moment to look down the hall at Annie's office and did not see a light on.

"She was here earlier this morning. I had a cup of coffee with her when I got here. She's probably just taking a tour around the place...she's been very busy lately. Yeah, I'm sure she's here."

Jay settled back on his heels. *She's not with him...that's a good sign. Maybe he just got cold feet about going to D.C.*

Hoffman relaxed a bit and signed off with his better half.

"His car is not here, he's probably not on a train then. He had to have come back here to get the car...unless someone else picked it up to use. He might be headed back to his house or the museum. Strange that he would ditch Summers though...is he onto us?"

He jogged the three blocks back to the precinct, his breath visible as he puffed the last half block. Checking with dispatch, he found that the sedan was not at Brian's house and that Annie could not be found within the museum. He didn't panic too much, he trusted Kit's opinion more than the rookie officer that he had sent over to the museum. It was beginning to appear that Brian's temporary disappearance was probably no big deal.

Hoffman didn't want to overreact and look like a foolish rookie. He would wait, check with the officers, and consult with Summers when he would return from Hastings. It was time to stay cool, time wasn't a critical factor yet if things were working as he thought. Deep in his stomach he felt a pit of worry though; he couldn't afford to be wrong on this one.

Chapter Twenty Nine

"They might not be onto us yet." - Brian Konrad

Brian and Annie knew that they could make Duluth shortly after one o'clock. They also felt confident that the police wouldn't start their search until they were partially up the north shore of Lake Superior. If they could cross the border near Thunder Bay their possibility of a clean getaway would go up significantly. They had to make the border before an all-points bulletin went out from Minneapolis.

With no time to lose, Brian pushed the sedan slightly over the speed limit as he passed through Pine City on Highway 61. They wouldn't need to stop, Annie had packed food for lunch and dinner if necessary. They had plenty of money. They knew of a safe motel on the south side of Thunder Bay if they chose to stop, otherwise they could push all the way to Sault Ste. Marie on the northeast end of Lake Superior.

Stopping briefly at Hinckley for gasoline and a bathroom break, Brian surveyed the area and saw no police. *A possible good sign...they might not be onto us yet.*

The car was running very well, they had heat and comfort and were enjoying each other's company on the trek. *"We can make it."* he reflected with a smile on his face.

Ten minutes later they were back on the two-lane highway and before they knew it, they were descending toward the huge Great Lake on the outskirts of Duluth. They gazed out at the large lift bridge and canal area with large ships, passed through the vibrant downtown, and left the beautiful port city in their rearview mirror. One checkpoint cleared, now on to Thunder Bay.

Back in Minneapolis, Summers had returned from Hastings and had given all the details of the slip. He made sure to let Hoffman know that to the best of his knowledge there had been no contact with Dr. Brooks in New York...there was a good possibility that the Soviets had no idea of Brian's plans or predicament. Keeping the Communist spies out of the equation was a positive thing...the aftermath of Brian's capture would go easier without negotiation.

After dismissing Summers, the young detective went back to working the museum angle. He drove over to MMA and met with Kit shortly after one in the afternoon. Greeting Kit with a kiss and a warm embrace near the office area, Jay got down to the pressing business. "Have you seen Annie since we talked last?"

Kit thought for a moment, looked up and down the long corridor, and replied quietly "I haven't seen her since about eight this morning. I thought she was just busy leading tours, but she was nowhere to be found at lunch. I'm not sure if she is here."

Hoffman's heart dropped, they might have a huge head start on him and he couldn't begin to guess where they were going. "Can you make an emergency announcement within the building?"

The announcement came over the loudspeaker, shattering the calm atmosphere in the building. Five minutes turned into ten and there was no sign of the pretty tour guide. "She's not here, is she?" he volunteered meekly, hoping Kit would have a better answer.

"Probably not. She always answers."

He looked down at his feet. "Damn it...they might have taken off."

Kit was puzzled and the couple retreated to her work area. Jay told her all about the situation but she refused to believe him, it just couldn't be true. As he wound his way through the whole story, she became a reluctant believer and, with tears welling in her eyes, she pledged her help with his cause. Jay promised to call her with any new developments and he hustled back to his headquarters in the heart of the city.

****

Konrad pulled the sedan off to a side street in a remote area of Silver Bay, a small town north of Duluth, and changed the license plates on the car. He had brought a set that had been removed from his next-door neighbor's car, knowing that he would only need them a short time and that his friend wouldn't even notice them missing.

As he changed the plates, Annie tucked her red hair up under a dark wig, checking herself in the rearview mirror to make sure no red was showing. Brian returned to the cab and laughed at her changed appearance. "You know you're sexy as a brunette, right?"

She purred back "Have you ever made it with a brunette before?" An image of Evie flashed briefly in his mind.

His eyes lit up at her suggestion and he chuckled "NO COMMENT!" as they rolled back onto the main street of the town.

Afternoon turned to evening and, although the days were now getting longer in Minnesota, Konrad knew that traveling by night was an advantage that he needed. Jay Hoffman had put out an all-points bulletin and teletype machines were chattering away, but it took time to get information statewide.

The machine in the Canadian customs lodge was chattering away, but the guards checked it infrequently as more often than not it was just daily events from across the globe. Brian and Annie reached the checkpoint to find both guards working at two cars ahead of them. As the cars passed, both men walked up and greeted them through the open window.

"Good afternoon. Where ya headed?" the older, gray haired guard on Brian's side of the car asked politely.

"We are on our way to Thunder Bay for our honeymoon." Konrad replied with a proud smile and a nod toward Annie.

"Well, Congratulations!" the guard offered with an honest grin. "How long do you plan to stay?" he questioned, per protocol.

"We will only be here for a couple of days...have to be back by the weekend."

The elderly guard had dealt with many of these newlyweds in his career, these two seemed perfectly normal. He spent an extra moment admiring the beautiful brunette in the passenger seat and gave the driver a knowing wink.

"Enjoy your stay. Congratulations again." he offered in his Canadian accent.

Brian smiled and pulled slowly through the checkpoint. They were about a quarter mile down the road when Annie moved close to him and put her arms around his neck. She laid her head on his shoulder and smiled, content and safe. Konrad echoed the sentiment, feeling victorious himself for the time being. The checkpoint was a major obstacle and they passed it with flying colors.

Back at the border station it was probably a half hour before the guards settled back into their small building and started checking the teletype. The younger guard spotted the all-point bulletin first and read it off to the old man.

"A couple, huh?"

"Yes, says here they are late twenties, early thirties, light complexions, female with red hair, dark sedan, license number JKE670 Minnesota plates. Did you take any plate numbers?"

The old man thought for a moment. *There had to be ten couples come through today. Plate numbers? Too much work. There were the newlyweds...she was brunette, very pretty...very pretty!*

He looked back at the rookie and replied confidently "Nope, no plate numbers, nobody that fit that description." As the young guard continued his dialogue the old man pondered the attractive couple a little more.

The travel became increasingly difficult for the couple as they trekked north toward the Canadian city of Thunder Bay. The roads were very dark and poorly kept, this made Brian sit up and pay closer attention to his driving. For the first time all day he now felt fatigued in both mind and body. Both of them needed a good night's sleep, but they wouldn't get relief until they reached the southern edge of the city.

Konrad struggled and Annie tried to keep him awake with conversation, but his mind was worn to an almost painful state. He tried not to be too short with her, but he was growing increasingly uncomfortable. The lights of the oncoming cars were making his eyes burn and his head hurt. At the moment where he felt like he was about to snap they recognized the lights of the city up ahead.

Brian pulled into the modern motor lodge and paid for the night in cash at the office. After a quick unloading of luggage from car to room, they both changed clothing and settled into a deep slumber while wrapped up in each other's arms. Having set an alarm for five o'clock in the morning, they picked up a solid seven hours of sleep and were cheery as they showered and prepared for the next leg of their journey. Little would they realize that they had just completed the easiest day of their getaway.

****

Brian and Annie were up and on the road before the sun came up. They started their trek along the north side of Lake Superior, not sure exactly where they were headed. In their limited plans, they had calculated that Toronto would be a safe haven and so they moved east across Canada. Konrad had thought about heading west to Edmonton and beyond, maybe all the way to Siberia, but he knew there would be more sympathizers and a better communication network if he headed east. The couple on the run had little debate over this topic, they both knew that the Soviet headquarters in New York City could provide them safe cover.

As the sun came over the horizon, the sedan pulled into a small gas station in the remote town of Nipigon. Brian refueled and then used the phone booth near the street to contact Dr. Brooks in New York City. He had been hesitant to disclose his plans up to this point because of Summers...he didn't need another tag along on this trip. Konrad figured that keeping Annie happy on this trek would be work enough; he had even considered going alone but could not leave her behind. Brooks answered his phone and was a bit surprised to hear his young protégé on the other end.

"Andrew. Brian here. I don't have a lot of time to talk."

The old man interrupted Konrad, ignoring the desperation in his voice. "Brian, how are you? I'm guessing you got your letter, right?"

Despite the cool morning air, beads of sweat were forming on the young curator's brow and he didn't have time for small talk. "Listen, I have to talk quick. Annie and I are headed out to the coast...we're in Canada now...we crossed over at Grand Portage."

The old man interrupted again. "What in the world did you do that for? Why?"

Brian continued right over his bosses' voice. "We are heading east and need refuge in case the Feds or Mounties start after us." The old man was quiet now, but mad at the couple for making such a bold move.

"We need to talk much more about this, but you continue heading east and I will set something up for you near Toronto. Stay safe and keep moving."

The young spy started breathing again. "Thank you, I will call soon, in a couple of hours maybe." Brian hung up the phone with a little less worry in his mind. Annie was waiting patiently as he climbed back into the car.

"Brooks says we need to head toward Toronto, we were right. I am supposed to call him in a couple of hours."

As the sedan pulled back onto the two-lane road and headed into the sunrise, a young agent sat at his desk in Upper Manhattan and transcribed the conversation word for word. He had been running surveillance on the Soviet safe house in Midtown for over a month, listening into conversations and recording everything.

Although he couldn't see much from his room directly across the street and eight floors up, he could tap into almost any conversation coming in or out of the complex. A group of four agents rotated over the course of every week, covering every minute of every day. The Feds knew they had found something special and were now working to figure out all of the programs initiated in the Communist world.

The FBI had learned through broken Soviet code and spies that this location was hot and it was yielding a treasure trove of good information. The studious agent stood up quickly at the end of the dialogue, made an additional note, and moved to the end of the room where his superior officer was working.

"Sir, I just picked this up from 50th street. You are going to want to read it right away." He handed the page to his boss and the agent studied it carefully. The senior C.I.A. agent picked up his phone and dialed the federal office in Minneapolis.

Chapter Thirty

"Everything is going to be alright." - Annie

The noise was almost deafening and the car began to shake violently as it veered to the shoulder of the bumpy road. It was pretty apparent that the Canadiens didn't think much of road maintenance. The ride had gotten so rugged that both Brian and Annie were starting to feel a little sick.

Now the car had failed them; a flat tire was the culprit. Brian got out, studied the flat at the front, and headed to the trunk for his needed supplies. Shuffling luggage about, he pulled the spare out of the trunk and went to work.

His status and inexperience showed, it took him over a half hour to make the tire change and stow away the ruined culprit. As he was putting things away a patrol car pulled in behind him. The Canadian Mountie approached with a stern look on his face, apparently his morning was starting rough as well. Brian displayed a weak smile and greeted the law man with a bit of nervousness.

"What seems to be the problem here, sir?" the Mountie inquired, not matching Konrad 's smile.

"Flat tire. Doggone road took it almost off the rim." he answered back somewhat short in reply.

"New one's on, aye?" The Canadian dialect put a smile on Brian's face.

"Yes sir, just getting on our way."

The Mountie studied the tire and then the woman in the passenger seat. His eyes lingered a bit too long and Annie stared back at him, breaking off his attention.

He moved around the car toward the back and halted with a look of concentration. "Minnesota, aye? What brings you up this way?" he turned and locked eyes with Brian. Konrad looked in at Annie for a second and then turned his attention back to the lawman.

"We're on our honeymoon, seeing the sights on our way to Toronto. My wife has a cousin there and so we're on our way to visit."

The lawman relaxed his posture and looked back at the woman in the car. "Very well then, enjoy your visit and drive safely, aye?"

Brian relaxed as well. "Thank you, sir. Have a nice day."

Konrad sat down in the driver's seat, looked behind him, and entered the single lane slowly. He didn't need any more attention, he just needed to get moving.

"Are you all right dear?" Annie asked with a caring tone.

"Yeah, just a little spooked by that cop. He wasn't any too friendly and was asking too many questions."

Annie slid over and cuddled against his arm to comfort him. "Everything is going to be alright." He gave her a smile as he drove on and slowly relaxed despite the horrible road. *"Everything is going to be alright."*

At about one o'clock the couple pulled into the tiny town of Wawa and found the only diner on the main street. They were both famished, their breakfast had been small and they were conserving the food they had in case of trouble.

The couple studied the clientele as they entered the greasy spoon and they found a booth near the front window. From here they could watch over their car on the street. The people in the diner studied them intently, knowing they were from out of town. The waitress came over, tried to make small talk, and took their order. Brian shut down the conversation, worried that she would learn too much about them.

A burger and fries arrived for him; Annie had a salad as she was conscious of her figure. The people in the diner seemed fixated on the two strangers. No one said anything to them, they just stared and whispered. Brian struck up a slightly louder than usual conversation with their waitress and boasted about their honeymoon trek across Canada.

This news lightened the mood and a few of the guests around them offered heartfelt congratulations. The couple beamed with pride, the perfect actors in this scene. When the time seemed right, Brian and Annie continued toward Toronto feeling confident that they were way ahead of the law.

****

Evie walked up the front steps of the precinct and found her way to Jay Hoffman's office. She was carrying her copy of the intercepted conversation from New York. Hoffman knew who she was, they had been corresponding on and off since her cover was blown earlier. Summers had put him on to her as well and now they would be working together.

The young agent took his time analyzing all of the information that was given to him by the female spy. He would work his way through all of the connections and conversations to piece together something that, until this point, he was totally unaware of.

Hoffman teamed Evie up with Summers, he figured that they would keep each other in check. He was pretty certain that he could trust Evie; Summers was another matter. He had flipped to the American side, but most Americans had a difficult time trusting anyone who had ever been affiliated with the Soviets. These were troubled times for America, one could never let their guard down. Mistrust chipped away at the young detective's mind, he could not afford to make a mistake and let Konrad get away.

Evie and Summers were sent to Toronto to intercept the runaway spies. The American network had little experience in working with Canada on a deal of this magnitude. Things were kept very quiet outside of the law enforcement circle; the news media was given no information about this case.

Departing from Minneapolis on a small charter plane, both American agents suffered a bumpy ride and finally found refuge in Toronto late in the day. Traveling as American policemen had its benefits, there were no worries of customs.

Evie and Summers settled in to adjoining rooms on the outskirts of the large city. Detective Hoffman would make the drive from Minneapolis, tracing the likely getaway route. He hoped to find enough information to culminate the trek with a victorious capture.

Chapter Thirty One

"Someone is watching me." - Summers

Summers was suddenly awakened from a deep sleep. The phone on the bed stand was ringing and it took thirty seconds for him to find it in the dark room. He picked up the phone expecting Evie from next door or Hoffman on the other end of the line.

"Yeah." he croaked hoarsely into the receiver. "You're a dead man. We know you turned. The curator makes it to Montreal or you're dead." The phone went silent, followed by the dial tone.

Holy shit...they know.

An icy chill ran through Summer's body as he sat up and dropped both legs over the side of his bed. "Damn it, I'm done."

Evie was sleeping soundly one door away. She was now a problem. Summers took a moment to get his bearings in the dark, went to the window, and opened the curtains to allow a sliver of sunlight to pierce the room.

"They figured me out, someone is tailing me right now. How in the hell did they get my room number?"

The older man was truly scared for one of the few times in his life.

Do I dare look out into the lot? They could snipe me in an instant. Wait, they won't yet, I have to deliver Konrad. Then they are going to kill me.

The realization that his game was about over was too much for him to handle; he fell back onto the bed and held his head as fear for his life overwhelmed him.

He needed Evie's help to catch the couple on the run. He couldn't ditch her; she was too sharp. Getting rid of her was out of the question. Hoffman had to be close, maybe a couple hundred miles out. Summers pondered the idea that Jay Hoffman could be of help to him if he were to get there in time.

Someone is watching me.

The thought kept running through his mind...it seemed endless and his stomach was now bothering him.

Quickly picking up his belongings and stowing them in his case, he left his room in shambles and knocked on Evie's door. She was ready to go for the day and as the door opened, he noticed how beautiful she looked.

"My, oh my, you look ravishing my dear!" he exclaimed before he could stop himself.

She returned a radiant smile and commanded "Let's go, they are probably already on the move."

She was all business, much to his chagrin. Evie realized how the Soviet network would protect their spies and she knew that time was of the utmost importance. If Konrad and Annie were to make Quebec the chase was probably over.

The Communist network was very quiet in Eastern Canada but was also deadly effective in protecting anyone they wished. She would have to catch them leaving Toronto and make a bold play to either apprehend them or kill them. She was hoping for the former and dreading the later, but she knew that either option was essential for her success. Summers was becoming more useless as the trek progressed, he was really nothing more than a diversion to keep boredom from driving her crazy.

If her calculations were correct, the fugitive couple could be holed up in Toronto, the police to the east had noticed no sign of the sedan with the attractive couple. They had numerous license plates to check and were on the lookout. She had checked for new information an hour earlier and was appraised of the situation.

A quick call to Hoffman had disclosed that he was trailing the entourage and would be in Toronto by noon. Her best option was to stake out the freeway to the East, they had to be headed for Montreal or Quebec City. Directing Summers, they moved out and stopped at restaurants and filling stations to ask about sightings of the couple. Two hours of questioning had turned up nothing.

The safe house that Dr. Brooks had given to Brian was six blocks south of the downtown area. Robert and Sandra Robinson were their hosts, the black sedan that the fugitives had driven was tucked away in their garage. A pleasant couple of about the same age as Brian and Annie, they provided the cover and company that was desired.

Both couples found they had plenty in common and it was decided that three or four days together would possibly clear some of the dangers posed by possible American pursuers. A change in vehicles could also take place here and Brian and Annie would be refreshed for the next phase of their getaway. All in all, it was a very pleasant interlude for the American runaways.

Summers and Evie were having no luck and she was getting crabby. Patience was never her strength, and now she had passed a point of no return. Her mood was getting downright ugly and Summers was bearing the brunt of every demand and criticism. She was not above placing blame on the older double agent; she was even moaning about the fact that he was probably working for the other side. Unless there was a spotting of the runaways, Summers would probably snap; the older man couldn't take any more of the female agents' nagging.

The only thing keeping Evie from killing her traveling partner was the arrival of Jay Hoffman. Leaving his government ride in Thunder Bay, he boarded a two-seater and flew the remaining distance to Toronto. The ride was like nothing he had ever experienced before and upon touchdown at the large airport he noticed that his shirt was soaking wet with sweat and his hands would not stop shaking.

Hoffman had arrived and he quickly checked in with the law enforcement agency downtown. Bulletins were distributed to the precincts and an information network was formed. If Konrad and Annie were anywhere near Toronto they would be captured.

Brian and Annie weren't near Toronto, they were *IN* Toronto. They realized that a network was being assembled to trap them, but they also knew that there were plenty of supporters working for them. It was time to put the next phase of the plan into action. The Robinsons dressed like the Konrads and with the proper makeup and hair dye, they were a spitting image of the runaways.

Robert and Sandra picked a nice, warm, Sunday morning to make their move. Law enforcement would probably be more relaxed on this day and time, it would be all the better to get moving again. Pulling the Konrad's car out of the garage, the

Canadian couple started moving west through Toronto at a normal speed. Waiting a half hour, Brian and Annie took the Robinson's gray Ford pickup truck out of the driveway and headed east out of Toronto.

Within twenty minutes of the first departure, the Toronto police had made contact with the Robinsons and had pulled them over on the main roadway west of the downtown area. Word spread quickly and Summers and Evie sped to the scene. Hoffman checked in downtown to await the arrival of the couple; he was beaming from ear to ear when he got the call.

The police took the Robinsons into custody thinking that they had Konrad and Annie. By the time Summers pulled up on the dark sedan the couple were already being transported to the police station. Evie harshly directed him to fall in and head to the main precinct where they could meet up with everyone.

"What in the hell!" she screamed, directing her wrath towards everyone in the room at once. Even the more experienced officers took a step back, overwhelmed with her anger.

"These are not the Konrads! How stupid can you be? You pulled the wrong people over!"

The disguise that the Robinson's had worn was good enough to fool the casual observer, but it was no match for anyone who really knew the fugitive couple. Summers made sure to keep his mouth shut as he feared she would shut it for him if he said a word. He could not, however, keep a smirk from his face as he admired the clever ruse that Brian had pulled off.

"Ma'am, this seems to be an honest mistake. They look just like the people you want and they were driving a car that matched the description."

Evie turned on the Canadian Mountie and lost her composure. With a fist to the chest that threw him off balance, she cursed loud enough for the whole city to hear.

Visibly frightened, all he could stammer was "Now, now...there will be none of that." Her eyes burned holes in him and he diverted his look from her to Summers, silently begging for help.

The female agent unleashed a verbal barrage on the Canadian agents.

"Let's get out of here. You idiots couldn't find your asses with both hands!"

Summers winced at this comment, understanding that the officers did the best they could. His hatred for Evie Katz was growing by leaps and bounds.

She stormed through the office portal, slamming the wooden door for effect, and made her way quickly to the car with hopes of getting back on the trail of Brian and Annie.

"That woman is a BITCH!" was all that the victim could state to his fellow mounties and they all broke out laughing at his misfortune.

Brian and Annie were wearing creative disguises. A little makeup, a touch of gray here and there, and they easily passed for a couple in their late forties out for a Sunday parlay to church. "So, this is how we are going to look at our twentieth anniversary, huh?" She chided him while running her fingers lightly through his hair.

"I will still think you are the sexiest woman on the planet!" he answered gently with a smile. Leaving town was easy, no one suspected anything. If they followed the rules of the road and obeyed the speed limit, they would be safe. It would take a minor miracle for any of the pursuers to catch them now.

Chapter Thirty Two

"This turned out to be a pretty good deal for you, huh?"
- Summers

Brian and Annie were making great time on their way east, they did not anticipate having to stop until Montreal or beyond. Their plans faced a sudden change when the truck began acting up near Ottawa. The engine stuttered and Konrad could feel the vehicle losing power. He pushed on, urging the truck to reach their destination, but it was not to be.

With a final shudder, the motor gave out and the truck rolled to a stop on the shoulder of the road. Despite being between two fair sized communities it felt as if they were in the middle of the wilderness. The couple gazed at each other with newfound despair.

It hadn't taken long for Evie and Summers to realize they had been taken. They sped east in pursuit of the fugitives, hoping to reach them before Montreal. The distance between the two couples changed from hours to minutes. Evie frantically pushed Summers to increase the pace; they were traveling at a dangerous speed. Summers knuckles were white as he worked to keep the vehicle on the pavement while his mind raced with the stress of the situation. He was fortunate; his car held up while Brian's did not.

They passed the abandoned pickup truck stranded on the side of the highway and didn't give it a second thought. Vehicles died all the time on these roads, out in the middle of nowhere. A mile down the road the Americans pulled into a service station to fill up on fuel and they were stunned by what they saw.

Brian and Annie had their backs to the gas pumps and were talking to a tow truck driver concerning their predicament. Summers recognized the silhouette of Brian first and he nudged Evie as he parked by the pump. Evie's jaw fell in disbelief, their targets had been reached.

Konrad handed the keys to the driver and the tow truck pulled out on the highway, travelling back from where they had all come. Dusky hues of an area remote masked Evie and Summers in their car by the pump.

Brian and Annie went inside the station's waiting area, looking to kill some time until the truck arrived. It was obvious to both that they would be spending the night and probably part of the next day while repairs were made.

Summers quietly backed his auto away from the pumps and around the corner where he could watch the couple without being detected. He had everything he could do to control Evie; she was losing her mind over wanting to apprehend the couple then and there.

Moving too quickly might expose Summers to the people who wanted to do him harm. He had to stall and look for the people who were watching him in order to save his own life.

"We have to wait until the right moment to apprehend them...he's got a weapon and she carries a small pistol as well. Be patient... we have them where we want them. He will kill you if you move on him too quick."

Evie thought the idea of Brian killing her was preposterous, Konrad was in love with her. It took more convincing by Summers to slow her down.

"Look, Evie. I know the man and I know how he has been trained. He knows we are chasing him...that's why he pulled a quick one on us back in Toronto. He has strict orders to kill anyone in his way...orders from Moscow."

He paused for effect, letting the words sink into Evie's mind.

"We will have an opportunity to take him without violence, trust me. The time will be right and we will be heroes."

The last comment settled the eager woman down and she smiled, trusting what she heard from the veteran double agent.

Brian and Annie started down the street toward a motor hotel two blocks away. There was hardly anyone around, the evening was quietly falling as they discussed what to do next.

Summers watched the couple enter the lobby of the lodge and then he moved his vehicle to the edge of the parking lot, staying as covert as possible. Evie was quiet now, waiting to pounce when the time was right. She had apparently deferred her power to Summers as she just stared wide-eyed at the scene.

The fugitives emerged after five minutes and walked their way toward the pursuers. The couple stopped about six doors down and Annie turned the key in the door. They entered the cozy room with Brian carrying a suitcase and a briefcase.

Summers and Evie quickly approached the office and gained a room and keys for themselves. They were lucky enough to get a room a couple of doors down from Brian and Annie, close but not too close. The motor lodge was shaped in an L and Summers room faced Brian's at an angle.

As Summers and Evie settled in, they found they could leave the curtains open a crack and see the door to Konrad's room; the perfect situation for surveillance. Summers made sure to park the car around the back, he didn't need Brian noticing the Minnesota license plates and getting suspicious. He took the first shift and Evie settled into a deep sleep on the bed.

As Evie slept soundly, a hundred thoughts raced through Summer's mind. He had to get rid of her, she could foil his plan to stay alive. At this point he was a man waiting to die, he had no idea when it would happen but he was sure it was inevitable. They were probably being watched at the same time he was watching Brian.

They would try to protect the fugitive couple anyway they could and if he didn't comply with the demands he would be eliminated along with Evie. He was in a difficult situation and it weighed heavily on his mind. Between his problem and the lust he felt for the demanding little spy sleeping soundly in the bed six feet away, he was about to go crazy.

Evie woke up at two a.m. and traded places with Summers. If he was lucky, he might get four hours of good sleep. He was tousled awake by the female fireball of energy at eight o'clock, fortunate to get six hours. The trouble was that the couple they were watching was now on the move back to the station and Evie wanted to intercept them as soon as possible. Brian and Annie passed by their window and Summers and Evie drew their weapons and made their move.

Opening the door quickly and stepping out onto the cement walkway, they were six feet behind the couple as they made their command.

"Freeze where you are or I'll shoot." Evie challenged in an evil voice, kept low to not gather attention.

Brian and Annie stopped and Summers continued.

"Slowly turn around with your hands over your head."

The couple slowly spun to face their captors and Brian's expression conveyed disbelief. He realized instantly that he had been apprehended by Evie and Summers. Annie was scared and confused, but did not utter a sound.

"Come here and step into the room." Summers ordered, his hand steady on his pistol. The stunned couple complied without a sound. Evie followed the group in and shut the door to the room. "Sit down on the bed and don't try anything funny...we will kill you."

Summers continued his directives in a low, menacing voice. He turned to Evie and ordered "Move over here and keep them covered. I need to tear up a bedsheet to secure them."

Evie held her weapon on the couple while Summers grabbed a pillowcase and tore it into strips. "Here, take this and tie her up first."

Evie was all smiles as she secured Annie with the pieces of cloth. She was aggressive, she wanted to scare and hurt the woman who had taken her man. With Annie incapacitated, she moved to Brian and started to tie him up.

The weapon came down over the top of her skull and she never knew what had hit her. Evie crumpled to the floor and Annie gave out a fearful whimper from behind her gag.

"What the hell Summers! What do you think you're doing?" Brian exclaimed, confused and angered at this aggression.

"She's here to take you into custody for the Americans. My job is to make sure you make it to the contact in Montreal before the Feds get you." Brian's face broke out into a wide smile as Summers continued.

"Dr. Brooks wants me to make sure you get to your destination. If you don't make it, I will be a dead man. This turned out to be a pretty good deal for you, huh?"

Summers turned toward the silent woman on the floor.

"Secure her. I don't think I killed her. We don't need her waking up right now. Tie her up."

Brian took the cotton strips and tied Evie's hands and feet together, she wasn't about to move anytime soon. Summers removed the restraints from Annie and the trio began to figure out their next move. Konrad took the last strip and used it as a gag on Evie; she was beginning to moan as she became conscious.

"I should just put a bullet in her head. Maybe just strangle her here. She's going to be a problem if we let her live. She'll come after us for sure. Besides, she's such a fucking nag."

Summers was working out his options out loud and Annie stepped back in revulsion. Summers looked from Annie to Brian, waiting for one of them to make the decision for him.

"Well? Should I off her?" he asked with an evil smile. Both of the runaways moved their heads back and forth with frightened looks on their faces. Evie could hear their voices.

God my head hurts! What the hell just happened? He's going to kill me? Play dead, just play dead and wait.

Evie was waking up and the throbbing behind her eyes was almost too much to bear. She fought to keep quiet and to keep her eyes closed.

Don't move, he will kill you.

"Let's not get crazy here, she won't catch up to us. The car will be out of the shop soon and we'll be on the road after I pay for the repairs. We're almost home free. She won't catch up, there's no sense in killing her."

She recognized Brian's voice and realized he was fighting in favor for her life. Despite the pain, she smiled slightly to herself.

He still loves me... he won't let me die.

"Let's get out of here. She's creeping me out and we have to go now if we are to get away." Annie was showing impatience and paranoia; they were so close to freedom.

"Yes... I will run down and get the car from the shop. She's not waking up. We'll pay for one more day of the room and we can hang the Do Not Disturb sign on the door. No one will know she is here. Let's GO."

Brian was also impatient; they were so close to a new life. "Ok, let's move."

Summers looked at Evie one more time, fought the urge to kick her in the head, and tucked his weapon away as they headed for the door in haste. Brian made sure to let Summers lead the way, he didn't trust the old spy alone with Evie, he'd kill her just for the fun of it.

Annie headed back to the front office and paid for an additional day of the motel room. Brian and Summers quickly walked around the back of the building to Summer's car and they drove down the street to get the repaired truck. Fifteen minutes later they were all back in front of the motel room.

"We should take both vehicles. I will need this after I deliver you in Montreal, or wherever we end up. Annie can ride with me so that you guys don't...get lost..."

Summer's words trailed off as he eyed the couple with suspicion. The realization that he needed them safe or he would be dead returned like a lightning bolt to his brain. Konrad wasn't about to let his bride out of his sight, he didn't trust Summers any more.

"Annie rides with me. We need you as much as you need us. We aren't going anywhere." Brian pulled Annie close and stared down Summers.

"Very well. Nothing funny. I'll follow you." The old man conceded, knowing he couldn't afford to cross the couple and make them mad.

Chapter Thirty Three

"This isn't over yet, you bastards!" - Evie Katz

The room was dark; the curtains were pulled tight so that no one could see inside. She was awake now and her head was throbbing with pain as she tried to assess her surroundings. She tugged gently at her wrist restraints, not wanting to tighten them any further. Her shoulders hurt almost as bad as her head, she was laying on her side and the pressure of her body had twisted her left shoulder awkwardly under her.

Using her abdominal muscles, she pulled herself up to a sitting position and started working her hands free. She had heard muffled voices outside and then heard two vehicles rumble away. With a little luck she would soon be free to rejoin the pursuit. *I just have to get my hands free.*

As Evie leaned back against the bed, still seated on the floor, she felt the edge of the metal bed frame jab her wrist. Moving her hands against the frame, she found the end and pushed her cloth restraint against it. Her work seemed futile and time was fleeting. After a tedious effort, she leaned with all her weight and the cotton strip gave way. *Yes! Yes!* She quickly removed her gag and breathed a sigh of relief.

"This isn't over yet, you bastards!" she exclaimed with a determined smile as she freed her legs and stood up to work the blood and feeling back into them. The fugitives had a head start on her and she would have to commandeer a car if she were to get back in the chase. With her legs working again and a throbbing bump on her head, she sprinted down the cement walkway to the main office.

Pulling out her credentials for the U.S. government, she startled the receptionist at the desk with her demand. "I need a dependable car right now! I will pay you for the car and gas. I need it now!"

The young girl behind the desk was barely old enough to drive, much less own a vehicle. She stammered with fear "My dad has a car...he owns the gas station down the street." Evie's mind was racing, she knew every minute counted.

"Give me your phone!" she shouted, reaching over the desk and snatching the receiver out of the desk clerk's hand. The young girl handed the rest of the phone to her and she dialed the number to the office back in Minneapolis.

Hoffman was out, a receptionist tried to transfer her call to someone on duty but had no luck.

"Doesn't anyone work anymore?!" she exclaimed as she slammed the phone down.

"Where's your dad's shop?" The young girl was on the verge of tears, visibly terrified of this crazy woman in her office.

"He's right down the street, back two blocks."

Evie recognized the location as the one that had fixed the broken-down truck the night before, the one that the fugitives were escaping with. She turned on her heels and ran out the glass doors, stopping only briefly to assess her situation.

"No phone contact, no vehicle, no Hoffman. They are getting away." Removing her high heels, she ran like a track star to the gas station.

Repeating herself from her encounter in the office two minutes ago, she had better luck with the station owner and found herself on the road in a small roadster five minutes later. She pushed the little car as fast as she could, almost hoping to get pulled over so that she would have assistance in the chase. She reached the outer limits of Montreal and located a pay phone with hopes of contacting Hoffmann.

With no sign of either the truck or sedan, her heart began to sink. *"Is it too late... Are they gone?"* It was the middle of the afternoon and she had no leads to follow and nowhere to look. She decided to drive around and see what she could find. The problem was that Montreal was a big city, much too big for her to explore in a day.

Brian, Annie, and Summers sat in a restaurant just off the main thoroughfare on the south side of the city. Night was falling and they had enjoyed very little to eat on this day. Realizing that the game was about over, they relaxed and ordered big. Confidence was high and they were feeling victorious! The warmth of the room, the light conversations around them, the exquisite food and drink, they were taking it all in with smiles.

"So, what now?" Summers asked in a relieved manner. Brian looked at Annie briefly and then decided to tell Summers the rest of the plan.

"Tomorrow we will check in to the safe office on Prince Edward Avenue. We can then negotiate asylum or catch a transport across the Atlantic. From there we will probably make our way to Moscow or Helsinki. One thing is for certain...life will never be the same."

He looked over at Annie and noticed the smile on her face. *"She's amazing...she'll follow me anywhere."* He flashed a knowing smile back at her and realized that their wedding would be in the near future.

"What are you going to do?" he asked Summers with genuine curiosity. Summers paused, looked down at his scotch, took a hard sip, and looked Brian in the eyes.

"I will probably reach out to Dr. Brooks again. I'd like to settle in the manor north of the city. It's safe, the government will protect me and the cops won't mess with me. From there it's all a mystery."

He smiled at the couple, but it was a nervous smile. He knew he wasn't in the clear. The Soviets could eliminate him for turning on them back in Minneapolis, or the United States could apprehend him and either give him life in Leavenworth or the chair.

Neither prospect appealed to him. The Soviet acceptance was his only hope, with the assistance of Dr. Brooks. Konrad noticed the tension and realized the heaviness of the situation that Summers was caught in.

"If there is anything I can do to help let me know." The offer was sincere and drew a smile from the older agent.

The couple picked up their belongings, paid the tab with a generous tip, and walked out to the parking lot. There was a chill in the air, the wind whispering around them as they made their way to their vehicles near the back. There was no reason for anymore small talk; they would head up the street to the Hotel Maxwell for a good night of sleep and then end the saga in the morning.

She stepped quietly out of the shadow of the diner, unseen by the trio until it was too late.

"Reach for a weapon and I will kill all of you." They halted and turned in her direction.

"One wrong move and you're all dead."

Summers jaw dropped when she walked out from the shadow as he realized his predicament. "Uh, Evie, uh..." The feisty agent took aim at him.

"Shut up or I'll put a bullet in your face." There was no tremble in her hand, the gun was steady and ready to be fired.

"You two, go get in your car and get the hell out of here."

Brian looked at Annie and then back at Evie. "What the hell are you waiting for? GET OUT OF HERE!" she demanded at the top of her lungs. Though shocked, Brian couldn't help but blurt out to her.

"What are you going to do with him? It's us you wanted, right?" Evie smiled at his chivalry.

"Back at the motel I heard everything you said. You saved my life. I think you still have feelings for me. Doesn't matter now...you have her. But you saved ME." She was almost blushing with joy as she revealed this. "I'll deal with you two later. Right now, it's all about Summers and me."

Brian and Annie turned toward their car and he looked back at Evie one last time. "Thank you." was all he could muster, somewhat relieved and yet choked up. They jumped into the truck and rolled out of the lot quickly. Evie focused all of her attention on her captured adversary.

"You're so stupid, you know that. You are an idiot! You turned on me when you should have taken them. Do you know how much trouble you are in?"

The old agent wanted to plead for his life or at least explain his situation, but fear took hold of his brain. He turned on his heels and sprinted toward the nearest cars, hoping to take cover.

She can't be a good enough shot to hit me on the run.

It was the last thing to go through his brain before the bullet did. She hit him with one shot, right in the back of the head.

Evie was surprised that she got him on the first one, but he wasn't very fast and ran straight away. A quick sense of pride filled her before she realized that he was face down and dead twenty feet away. The diner emptied with the gun shot and commotion filled the parking lot. She pulled her credentials and the authorities were summoned. Three royal policemen in squad cars arrived within two minutes.

Entering inside to the warmth of the restaurant with a policeman, she explained that two of the fugitives had gotten away and she was forced to put down the third. The lawman radioed a description of Brian and Annie to the station for an all-points bulletin to be issued. Evie found herself surprisingly calm considering this was the first person she had ever killed in the line of duty. It helped to know that he had wanted to kill her and he had turned on his country.

The cop returned to her booth. Evie had no knowledge of the city and needed a place to stay for the night. "Do you know of a good hotel around here...I'll probably be here for a couple of days."

He looked her over, wishing he could spend a couple of days and nights with her. "Um, the Hotel Maxwell is right down the street. I can take you there if you wish." He was inviting the possibility of getting to know her better.

She brushed him off for now, there was too much to do. *"Maybe some other time..."* she mused to herself with a smile. He did appeal to her, she sensed they could have plenty of fun.

"I have my own ride outside, but thanks for the offer."

Not to waste an opportunity, the young officer replied "Just call the precinct if you need ANYTHING. I am James Stonestreet...at your service." He flashed a killer smile at Evie and she almost took him up on his offer.

It was after eight o'clock when she finally reached Jay Hoffman by phone. He was surprised by the events that had unfolded; the Canadian police had filled him in on the details of the shooting before Evie could reach him.

"Did you see Brian and Annie up there?" he quizzed, hoping for an affirmative answer.

"No, they were nowhere to be found. I got lucky and ran into Summers, he had turned on us. I had no choice but to fire on him, he was drawing on me." She threw the little lie in there to make things more acceptable.

"Do you think they are near?" he pushed, hoping for a chance at the couple.

"I don't know, it seemed as if Summers was looking for them too. I don't think he was having much luck."

"What makes you think that Summers was working against us?" he questioned slowly, looking for logic in the situation.

Evie paused and weighed the question in her mind.

"He ran from me and chased them, but he turned on me when I caught up. He was going to eliminate me to save them. It was just a feeling I had and then, when he drew his weapon on me in the lot, I had to act quick." She paused again, hoping he was buying the story.

"He knocked me out and tied me up at the motel near Ottawa." Stunned silence occupied the line for a moment.

"He did WHAT?!" Hoffman shouted, startled by this revelation. "How come you didn't call me?"

Evie was nervous now, but her story covered her fear. "I tried to call you...I tried and tried, but no one knew where you were. It all happened so fast." Silence again. She was extremely calm considering the events that had transpired in the last twelve hours; she had to work hard to sound shaken by what had taken place. The damsel in distress hoped Hoffman was buying her tall tale.

"My god, Evie, he could have killed you. Are you OK? Should I come to Montreal now? I'm not that far away." The lead detective blurted his concern, scared for the safety of Evie. She waited a moment, trying to figure out how to handle this.

It would be helpful to have Hoffman here...

She broke the silence with reassurance.

"Don't worry, they are probably not even here. I'm alright, you can come out if you want but it's probably not a big deal." He didn't waste much time in making his decision.

"I will be there tomorrow. Will you be ok until then?" She paused and then responded.

"I am staying at the Hotel Maxwell, room 421. Call me when you get here."

"Evie, please listen to me. Don't try to apprehend them by yourself. One day won't make a big difference, for all we know they are already gone. If it's meant to be, we will catch them tomorrow...just wait for me, will you?"

He was almost pleading, hoping she could be patient enough to allow him to catch up.

"Don't worry, Jay. I will wait for you. It will be one hell of a boring day, but I will wait for you."

They both chuckled lightly at her humor and signed off with a good night. Hoffman made plans to get to Montreal as quick as he could. Then he placed a call to New York City.

Chapter Thirty Four

"I think everything has fallen into place the way it should." - Jay Hoffman

Hoffman had traveled the dark Canadian roads from village to city and arrived at the Hotel Maxwell as the sun was rising. Having composite pictures of both Brian and Annie, he was stopping at restaurants and hotels along the way.

As he entered the plush lobby of the Maxwell a hunch came over him and he took the pictures from his breast pocket. He approached a plump woman of middle age who looked weary from the night shift and he laid the pictures and his badge on the counter.

"Good morning. My name is Detective Hoffman of the United States Federal Bureau of Investigation, and I am wondering if these two people look familiar to you. Perhaps with different hair color?"

He paused a moment as she smiled and looked down at the photos. A look of intense concentration replaced her smile as she studied the pictures.

"You know, it was pretty slow last night, but they kind of look familiar. Different hair color maybe?" She paused and pondered their appearances further. Hoffman was starting to get a little impatient, he was also tired and longed for some shut-eye.

"I think they checked in last night, around eight or nine o'clock. They were a couple and they were in a bit of a rush. Pleasant people though. I'm almost sure it's them." She looked up with a satisfied smile, thinking she had accomplished something big.

"The man was more grey than this...he looked a little older. The woman had darker hair. But, you know, I think it may have been them."

Hoffman looked her in the eyes and with an official whisper and a charming smile posed a riskier question.

"You wouldn't happen to be able to tell me what room they are in, could you? Official business, of course."

The compliant receptionist looked up and down the counter, checked the room log, and whispered back in her most covert manner.

"They are in room 223, up the stairs to the right." She was intrigued by his status and demeanor and returned his smile with intense interest.

"Thank you, ma'am, you have been a great help." His wink generated a blushing complexion from the night clerk and he strode with an extra spring in his step to the elevators.

Hoffman knew deep in his mind that he had them, that this was shaping up to be a great day. Now he had to make contact with Evie. She had no idea that she was staying in the same hotel with Konrad ...the overzealous agent would no longer be needed and would be a hindrance.

He took the lift up to Evie's room and gently knocked on the door. There was no noise coming from the other side. He felt a wave of embarrassment and guilt roll over him; he was probably waking her up. He paused and then turned back toward the elevator; he could head down to the coffee shop and wait until she was up and about. The detective ordered a steaming cup and sat down to check the morning headlines in the local newspaper.

The woman appeared in the doorway and startled him for a moment, he had absolutely nothing to say. To the people seated at tables around him, they would have seen a noticeable drop of his jaw. He raised the paper higher to cover his identity and peered over the top of the headlines.

She strolled with quiet caution to the main counter and engaged in conversation with the waitress; she was smiling the whole time. It had to be her. He couldn't hear what she was saying and he assumed it was an order for food or drink.

"She looks different." he quietly thought out loud.

The woman turned her head in his direction and he raised the paper higher to conceal his identity. He waited for a moment and then peeked over the top. She had turned away, not recognizing him.

He watched the waitress place two croissants in a paper bag and hand them over the counter along with two cups of coffee in paper cups. She took the goods and turned quickly toward the door. Hoffman gently folded the paper, placed it on the table in front of him, and followed her at a discreet distance.

Annie carried the goods to the elevator and, with a little bit of difficulty, pushed the button for the second floor. As the doors slid toward each other, Hoffman eased his way between the panels and looked her in the eyes. Annie's expression gave away the horror in her mind. A cup of coffee hit the floor and splattered at her feet.

"Hi Annie. What are the odds that we'd meet here?" he said with a grin, brimming with confidence.

"I'm...not...Annie." she stammered with a shaky voice.

"Give it up, the game is over. Let's go see Brian. Don't try anything funny, my weapon is loaded." His grin sent a chill down her back as she shrunk in defeat.

They paused at the door to 223. He whispered to her in a determined voice.

"Open it slowly, nothing funny." She turned the key and pushed the door open. Jay followed her into the room, weapon drawn at her back.

Brian was sitting in a chair near the window, looking out to the street. He turned and the expression on his face was one of stunned amazement. "Jay! What in the world are you doing here?" He couldn't contain his dejection and defeat. The game was over. Annie looked at Brian helplessly and began to cry.

"Sit down on the bed." Hoffman commanded with a threatening tone. Annie dropped to the side of the mattress.

"You, nothing funny." he ordered to Konrad. Brian and Annie's eyes met and he slowly moved over to sit next to her on the bed and comfort her.

A hush fell over the room. Brian broke the silence with curiosity.

"So... Jay, what now?" Hoffman looked both of them over and then glanced out the window, weapon still trained on the pair.

"Well, I think we will be meeting up with some people later today. Finding you here has put a plan into motion. We will be moving together, try anything funny and I will have to kill you. Your run comes to an end today. Do what I say and you will live to see tomorrow."

Hoffman's tone gave no indication of the friendship they had held. He was all business now.

"You know that Evie is in town, right?" Konrad mentioned, hoping to get some indication of where she was.

"She's here all right...two floors above us." the detective answered with a laugh. "She won't be a factor in what we do today, at least she shouldn't be."

Brian felt a small sense of relief come over him for in his mind Evie was a loose cannon, extremely emotional and dangerous to both Annie and him. Keeping her out of the situation gave him a small glimmer of hope.

Konrad's mind started processing the scenario.

Evie is here...he doesn't want to deal with her...why? It would be easier for him to have her help...is she holding Summers? We're so close...I have to find a way to make a break for it.

"Where's Summers?" Brian asked, hoping for more information.

"Summers is dead. Evie shot him last night at a diner down the street. She called me afterwards and asked that I get here as soon as possible. Here I am."

Hoffman looked the couple over. It was strange for him to comprehend this situation...a week ago they were all friends planning a wedding back in the Twin Cities. Now they were in another country facing a difficult situation that could be the demise of Brian and Annie.

"How come Evie isn't here with you?" the young curator asked as he built a getaway plan in his head.

"Don't need her. She's more work than I can handle right now. I went for a cup of coffee and came back with Annie! I think everything has fallen into place the way it should. Pack your bags and let's move...we'll take my car and you will drive. Now MOVE!" he commanded with impatience and authority.

Brian and Annie packed their belongings and were ready to go. Both seemed resolved to their fate. "We will take the stairs...no elevator. Any funny business and I will shoot you both. I have the law on my side...Canadian and American. Let's go."

The trio exited the room with their luggage and headed to the end of the hall. The exit was clearly marked and they descended the stairwell to the main floor. Stopping briefly to survey the situation,

Hoffman directed them away from the main lobby toward a side door that led into the parking lot.

"Don't scream or I will shoot. See the sedan over there with the Minnesota plates? That's where we are headed. You will place your luggage in the trunk and both get into the front seat. I will sit in back and direct you. Anything funny and it's all over for you."

The fugitives and their captor got into the sedan and began driving toward the highway. Hoffman held the weapon aimed at the front seat and gave directions as Brian steered the vehicle.

I can't create a commotion because it will gain the attention of the police and he's one of them. Can't disarm him, he's behind us...too dangerous. What can I do? Brian's mind was racing as he wasn't about to give up yet.

He looked over at Annie, she had barely made a sound. She looked terrified. He reached across the bench seat and took her hand in his. She squeezed back, and looked at him for reassurance that they would work their way out of this predicament. He nodded back with confidence as he drove. They both needed to be strong.

Chapter Thirty Five

"Spy is a harsh term." - Brian Konrad

The automobile made its way out of the city to the sparse countryside, alone in its journey away from Montreal. The sun of the morning felt warm in the car, it seemed to offer some unknown hope for the couple. They did not feel hopeful, instead they felt the dread of an impending doom.

With Hoffman's directions, they had put a good thirty miles on the odometer before they came to a remote intersection surrounded by fields of clover and dirt. They turned off the main road and continued as they began to climb slowly up the hilly terrain. The view of the countryside from above was captivating and Hoffman found himself stealing glances out of the side windows as they pushed on.

Despite being close to a large city, they were in a beautiful but remote rural area. With farmland sprawled below them, they finally came to a plateau and pulled off the road. A dirt parking area with a lookout perch was now their location and Brian was puzzled by this locale.

A small, whitewashed diner sat on the bluff, its large windows using the beautiful view below to its advantage. It appeared empty from the outside, but the OPEN sign was visible on the front door. Two cars sat up against the building near the back. Brian wondered to himself how an establishment like this in the middle of nowhere could stay open. His mind quickly returned to the problem at hand.

Hoffman led the couple into the building and they sat down at a window booth farthest from the door. If anything were to happen here, he made sure he could see the whole dining room. With Brian and Annie seated, he invited them to order. This struck the couple as strange and they exchanged puzzled glances.

"We're going to be here a while, pick out something good...my treat."

A young girl of about sixteen or seventeen approached the table to take their order. Hoffman stood up and approached the long counter that spanned the dining area.

"Can I use your phone to make a local call?" he asked politely. A large, balding man dressed in a well-worn apron handed the black dialer across the pink Formica countertop. Retrieving a card from his trouser pocket, he dialed the number that was listed and conversed with an official on the other end of the line.

The phone call lasted less than two minutes and the detective gave his whereabouts as best as he could. The man on the other end of the line knew exactly where he was; they had spoken before.

Brian and Annie, not wanting to take a chance on food poisoning, decided to go with the standard burger and fries. It was after nine o'clock at this point, but the young waitress didn't think that an early lunch would be a problem. She left with their order and the cook disappeared into the back kitchen to go to work.

Hoffman sat down and eyed the two captives with an air of curiosity and compassion. He didn't know what their future held and he was pretty certain that this would be the last time he would ever see them. They had grown close as friends back in Minneapolis and he felt a little sad as he pondered the end of their friendship.

The couple had deliberately chosen not to talk, they were afraid that anything they said could come back to haunt them. They sat in captive silence and the food arrived within fifteen minutes. Having had a feast the night before, they picked away at small morsels slowly. The situation that they now found themselves in took away the desire to eat much and so most of the food went untouched.

Annie kept looking at Brian for any clue of what to do and she had to work hard to not cry out loud. With a good amount of effort, the detective finally got Brian to open up about who he was and what had really been happening back home.

The curator felt there was nothing to lose at this point and opened up to Jay about his getaway plan.

"That was pretty creative, and you almost pulled it off. Ditching Summers at the station really had us going." Both men smiled and let out a quiet chuckle.

"Our time together is just about over. Authorities are on their way to meet you and I will be leaving you here. Off the record, what was going on in Minneapolis? Are you guys really spies?" Hoffman voiced his question with friendly concern. The tone in his voice and the memory of their friendship caused Brian to open up.

"Spy is a harsh term." You could say I was a conduit between groups of people...a middle man of sorts." Hoffman leaned an elbow on the table, more curious as Konrad continued. "Annie had nothing to do with any of this. She really doesn't know much if anything about the project. She's my lover, not a fellow accomplice. Summers was involved with me and, according to you, he's now dead."

The detective nodded and waited in silence as Brian chose his words carefully.

"I moved stuff through the museum, coast to coast you could say. I don't know much of what was in the crates. I just followed the order forms and sent stuff on its way."

Brian was telling his friend some minor white lies, afraid of consequences if the story were to get back to the States. Hoffman followed the words with interest but knew there was much more that he wasn't being told. The young detective had basically put the whole story together and had gathered much of it from Summers earlier. Jay played it cool and did not let on to the fact that he knew the whole scheme. He quietly let Konrad continue.

"The Rosenberg thing really shook me up. I don't want to end up in the electric chair." Annie let out a small gasp and a shudder that was visible to both men. Brian placed his hand on hers for reassurance and support.

"Things got crazy and Summers suggested that I stop. Then Washington D.C. sent out the summons and I panicked. They are hunting for anyone and everyone...I'd never have a chance with them. So we decided to make a run for it, a new beginning. Something we could no longer have in the States."

Jay shifted in his seat and looked at both of the captives.

"How do you know you couldn't have a life back home?" Brian looked at Annie and then back at his friend across the table.

"Come on, you know as well as I do that if they got me in D.C. they would probably never let me go. It's a witch hunt and you are guilty until you prove your innocence. No one gets out alive when you get to this stage. They say Rosenberg's wife had nothing to do with his plan, she didn't know a thing, and now she is a goner. We'd be dead in a year if we went to D.C. or stayed in the States. This was the only alternative...there are people here who can help us."

Silence settled over the booth; Jay didn't know what to say. He felt sorry for his friends and felt a twinge of regret at the fact that he was on the other side of the law from them. His mind flashed to Kit back home and all the good times that the two couples had shared. Those times would be no more. A black sedan pulled up next to the diner and two very large men in dark three-piece suits got out.

The strangers surveyed the surroundings with an air of official business and then entered the diner with a deliberate demeanor. One or two guests had sauntered in and now were eyeing the men with a wary concern. The powerful men paid the guests no attention and went directly to the occupied booth at the back. They stopped at the edge of the table and quietly eyed the trio. No one said a word for what seemed like an eternity.

"Mr. Brian Konrad?" With a low, deep voice, the older of the two men directed his question at Brian. Konrad fearfully returned the gaze and nodded, realizing that the escape had come to an end. Annie leaned over to him and rested her head on his arm.

"You, get out."

The man pointed to Hoffman and the detective slid out of the booth, following the second black suit out of the building. The first big man slid into Hoffman's spot and looked the couple over with a smile. Konrad directed his gaze out the large window and saw their belongings being transferred from Hoffman's sedan into the black car. *All this way and so close to freedom...now it's over.* The young curator's shoulders sank with defeat.

"Mr. Konrad, I am here as a representative of an acquaintance of yours...a Mr. ABE." Brian's head jolted back from the window view to the big man across from him. Shock filled his mind and Annie was surprised by the violent jolt.

"Excuse me...what did you just say?" was all Konrad could muster in a stammered form.

"Mr. Konrad, I represent Mr. Abe... I believe you know him? We are here to take you to safety."

The captive couple could not believe what they had just heard, the comment was so unbelievable that it took a minute to set in. "So, you are not from the

C.I.A, F.B.I, the United States? You are not with Hoffman?" The big man smiled, knowing that the couple was in the dark with what was now happening.

"I take it Mr. Hoffman has told you nothing. Very well. Very good. My name is Alex and you will be coming with me and my associate, Paul. We will be taking you to the next step in your journey. Do not be afraid, the most dangerous part of your removal is probably over…knock on wood as they say in your country." With that statement the big man smiled again and knocked on the table for superstitious effect.

Annie started tearing up with joy and Brian hugged her, knowing that things had taken an unexpected turn for the better. Relief flooded their emotions, they felt as if all the weight in the world had been lifted from their shoulders.

The big man slid to the end of the seat and stood up with authority. An imposing figure, he commanded everyone's attention solely on his appearance and mannerisms.

"Come with me, it is time to go."

The couple slid out of the booth and followed their newfound colleague out of the front door.

The warmth of the mid-morning sun shone down on their faces and the spring breeze graced their senses in a way that they had never felt before. It was great to be alive, great to have hope for tomorrow. Alex led them to the dark auto and opened the door for them. The couple stood in the warm breeze, feeling like they were reborn. Brian looked back at the automobile across the parking lot.

Jay Hoffman sat behind the wheel, showing no emotion. Paul stood outside the driver's side window and a thick, white envelope was passed to the detective. Alex waited for them to get into the car and Brian suddenly turned toward the other vehicle.

Annie followed her man as he walked with a purpose toward the detective; she felt fear overtake her for a moment. The younger comrade stepped aside as Jay opened his door, stood up, and walked to the front of his vehicle.

Konrad came to a sudden stop three feet away from his friend. Annie halted with a bit of a stumble behind him. Both men surveyed each other silently.

"I don't understand." was all that Brian could mutter. "You don't need to know. I know the whole story, even the stuff you didn't tell me in there." Brian's eyes dropped with guilt.

"Don't let it worry you, I know why you didn't tell me everything. I didn't tell you everything either... I couldn't." Konrad looked back up at his friend, compassion in his eyes.

"How did you turn? Did you call these guys?" he asked with confusion.

"You don't need to know any of that. It could get both of us killed." Hoffman shared in a low tone with a bit of a laugh. Both men smiled and Brian moved toward the detective with a manly embrace.

Sadness overtook them as they took mental note of the end of their friendship.

"Thank you...thank you." Brian muttered with a solitary tear in his eye.

"Don't mention it...just go."

Brian backed up and Annie moved forward to embrace their friend. With a quick hug and a kiss on the cheek she retreated and both turned back to the car across the lot. After about a dozen steps, Brian heard his friend call his name.

"Konrad." He pivoted a quarter turn and looked back at the detective. Jay Hoffman called out with strength in his voice and a gentle smile. "We will meet again, friend. We will meet again."

Brian smiled a hopeful smile, turned, put his arm around Annie, and they walked to the waiting car and a new world.

The End

About The Author

D.J. Hamlin is a published writer through Northern Star Publishing and "The Middle Man" is his first novel. Specializing in historical fiction, this work is the first in a series. A second novel, " A New World " is expected for release by the end of 2019. In addition to the series, the author has also written a stand-alone novel that should be on shelves soon. When not writing, D.J. teaches Social Studies and coaches football in the beautiful state of Minnesota.

Coming Soon: Brian and Annie face a whole new challenge a half a world away... "Half A World Away", Book Two of the Brian Konrad series premiering in late 2019!